No Big Easy

Longarm struggled through the brush. The vines and creepers almost seemed to be alive and striving to hold him back. Finally—and somewhat to his surprise—he burst out of the undergrowth and stumbled onto the trail where he had left Natalie.

He heard her scream. She ran out of the trees on the far side of the trail from Bayou Noir. A man lunged after her, reaching for her. Longarm brought up his Colt.

She screamed, "Custis! Look out!"

Too late, he tried to turn as he realized the real threat was behind him. A huge weight crashed into him. When he hit the trail, he drove an elbow up and back and felt the point of it sink into a man's belly. The man who had tackled him grunted in pain.

There were at least two enemies here, the one who had tackled him and the one who had chased Natalie out of the trees. That man had caught her, Longarm saw now. She was struggling to break free. Before Longarm could reach his gun, more men stepped out of the concealment of the trees. At this range, they could blow him to shreds without any trouble . . .

TABOR EVANS

LONGARM

**AND THE BAYOU
TREASURE**

JOVE BOOKS, NEW YORK

THE BERKLEY PUBLISHING GROUP
Published by the Penguin Group
Penguin Group (USA) Inc.
375 Hudson Street, New York, New York 10014, USA
Penguin Group (Canada), 90 Eglinton Avenue East, Suite 700, Toronto, Ontario M4P 2Y3, Canada
(a division of Pearson Penguin Canada Inc.)
Penguin Books Ltd., 80 Strand, London WC2R 0RL, England
Penguin Group Ireland, 25 St. Stephen's Green, Dublin 2, Ireland (a division of Penguin Books Ltd.)
Penguin Group (Australia), 250 Camberwell Road, Camberwell, Victoria 3124, Australia
(a division of Pearson Australia Group Pty. Ltd.)
Penguin Books India Pvt. Ltd., 11 Community Centre, Panchsheel Park, New Delhi—110 017, India
Penguin Group (NZ), 67 Apollo Drive, Mairangi Bay, Auckland 1311, New Zealand
(a division of Pearson New Zealand Ltd.)
Penguin Books (South Africa) (Pty.) Ltd., 24 Sturdee Avenue, Rosebank, Johannesburg 2196,
South Africa

Penguin Books Ltd., Registered Offices: 80 Strand, London WC2R 0RL, England

This is a work of fiction. Names, characters, places, and incidents either are the product of the author's imagination or are used fictitiously, and any resemblance to actual persons, living or dead, business establishments, events, or locales is entirely coincidental.

LONGARM AND THE BAYOU TREASURE

A Jove Book / published by arrangement with the author

PRINTING HISTORY
Jove edition / May 2007

ISBN: 978-0-515-14300-3

JOVE®
Jove Books are published by The Berkley Publishing Group,
a division of Penguin Group (USA) Inc.,
375 Hudson Street, New York, New York 10014.
JOVE is a registered trademark of Penguin Group (USA) Inc.
The "J" design is a trademark belonging to Penguin Group (USA) Inc.

PRINTED IN THE UNITED STATES OF AMERICA

10   9   8   7   6   5   4   3   2   1

Chapter 1

Murky water splashed high as Longarm ran through the swamp. He heard the hounds baying behind him. The pursuit was closing in, but he didn't try to be stealthy in his flight. He continued making as much noise as possible.

He wanted the men and the dogs to stay on his trail, rather than going after the others.

From the sound of it, his plan to draw the pursuers away from his companions was working. The hounds were closer now, and when Longarm paused to draw in a couple of deep lungfuls of the foul, humid air, he heard men shouting to each other, too.

His mouth stretched in a humorless grin. The fingers of his hands crooked a little in his desire to clamp them around the neck of one of those bastards.

Vengeance would have to wait. It was more important that his companions have every possible chance to get away without being caught.

He started running through the swamp again, hoping that he wouldn't step right on a cottonmouth or coral snake or gator. Trailing vines tugged at him, tried to hold him back like clutching hands. Tree roots extended under the water and threatened to trip him if he wasn't careful.

He couldn't afford to be too cautious, because that would slow him down. He wanted to draw off the pursuit, sure, but he also wanted to get away himself.

If he didn't escape, he couldn't come back to deliver justice to this godforsaken marshy wilderness.

When he glanced over his shoulder he saw movement through the screen of brush. The pursuers were really close now. Longarm spotted a hummock covered with tall grass. Time to go to ground, he decided.

He climbed onto the hummock and plunged into the grass. It closed in around him as he stretched out on his belly. If he was very still and didn't cause the grass to wave around him, maybe the pursuers would go on by and then he could double back to rejoin the others. The ground was damp underneath him, but that didn't really matter since his boots and the trousers from his brown tweed suit and the once-white shirt he wore were already soaked and covered with mud from his flight through the swamp.

He forced himself not to gasp for breath. Since he was more accustomed to the dry, crisp air of the high country, he didn't like this moist lowland atmosphere. But it beat not having any air to breathe at all, he supposed.

As soon as he was still, mosquitoes began to buzz and hum around his ears. He felt them biting his face but couldn't move to brush them away. The pursuers were almost right on top of him now. The dogs seemed to have finally lost his scent, so that was something to be thankful for, at least. He heard the men complaining about "damn useless hounds."

Something rustled in the grass behind Longarm.

He risked a look over his shoulder and almost shouted in alarm. Less than ten feet from him, an alligator had poked its blunt nose out of the thick grass. The big leathery-hided creature waddled a couple of steps forward before stopping to regard him with its cold, soulless eyes.

Longarm's pulse hammered loudly in his head. He

clamped his jaws together as tightly as he could to keep from crying out. It was possible the gator might go on without bothering him, especially if there was other prey nearby to be had.

Like those two hombres who were now splashing through the swamp only a few yards away with a couple of bloodhounds.

The dogs suddenly started baying at the hummock, and one of the men said, "Damn, I bet he's up there! Let's take a look."

"Be careful," advised the other one. "We don't know if he's armed or not."

"Whatever he's got ain't gonna be no match for this scattergun."

As a matter of fact, Longarm wasn't armed. He had left the lone handgun with the others. So now he was caught with a gator behind him and a couple of hardened killers in front of him. Talk about a rock and a hard place.

He was sure going to have a bone to pick with Billy Vail when he got back to Denver. *If* he got back to Denver . . .

"I'm sending you to Louisiana," Billy Vail had said a week earlier as he faced Longarm over the desk in his office. Vail was the Chief Marshal for the Western District despite the fact that with his pink scalp and cherubic face he looked more like somebody's kindly old grandpa than a veteran lawman.

"Aw, Billy, you know I don't much like that country down there," said Longarm as he fished one of his three-for-a-nickel cheroots out of his vest pocket. "It's hot and sticky and they got voodoo and such-like."

"You're not going to New Orleans," Vail said.

"Still be hot and sticky," said Longarm as he snapped a lucifer to life with an iron-hard thumbnail and set fire to the gasper.

As if he hadn't heard the comment, Vail went on,

3

"You're going to a little town about halfway between Baton Rouge and the Gulf of Mexico. Place is called Saint Angelique."

Longarm blew a smoke ring toward the banjo clock on the wall of Vail's office. "What's in this Saint Angelique that requires the presence of a deputy U.S. marshal?"

"It's the last place where a fella named Matthew Chadwick was seen before he headed out into the swamp."

Longarm frowned. "Some fella gets swallowed up by the swamp, and you're sending me all the way to Louisiana to look for him? Hell, Billy, he's probably in some gator's belly by now. Either that or the crawdads ain't left anything of him but bones."

Vail gave Longarm a meaningful look and said, "Senator Chadwick asked for you in particular, Custis."

The light dawned. Longarm said, "Ah."

Tobias Chadwick was a United States senator from Louisiana. Longarm had never worked on a case in which Chadwick was mixed up directly, but several of his assignments in the past had involved senators. Even though he didn't have much use for politicians, he had gotten a few of them out of some pretty bad fandangos. And senators were like anybody else—they had friends on the job, and when they ran into a problem they might ask those friends for advice.

"I reckon Matthew Chadwick must be Senator Chadwick's son or brother?" continued Longarm.

"Son," Billy Vail confirmed.

"And when he disappeared, the senator asked around the capital about somebody who could go and look for him."

Vail nodded. "And your name was mentioned more than once, I reckon, because Senator Chadwick went to friends of his in the Justice Department and asked that you be assigned to the case."

"I knew the last time I found some damn fool politician

4

twisting in the wind I should've just left him there," muttered Longarm. "Knew my generous nature would come back to haunt me someday."

Vail ignored that, too. He picked up a document from a welter of papers on his desk. "Says here young Chadwick thought that Jean Lafitte's treasure was hidden somewhere in the swamp near Saint Angelique. He was going to look for it."

Longarm's teeth clenched on the cheroot. He chewed it for a moment before he took it out and said, "If you recollect, I've gone chasing after pirate treasure before. Damn near got me killed, too."

"You're not looking for treasure in this case," Vail pointed out. "There may not even be any. You're looking for a fella who was looking for treasure."

Longarm resisted the urge to roll his eyes. Instead he said, "I thought pirates usually buried their loot on desert islands and such."

"Seems young Chadwick got his hands on an old diary that claimed Lafitte's treasure was hidden in the swamp. Lafitte operated in the Gulf of Mexico and had a hideout on the Louisiana coast. It's really not that far-fetched to think he might've gone inland to cache some of his ill-gotten gains."

"Maybe," said Longarm with a shrug. "So you don't care about the treasure; you just want the senator's son back."

Vail nodded. "Safe and sound if you can manage it." A grim expression settled over his normally pleasant face. "But even if you can't, the senator still wants to know what happened to his boy."

Longarm sighed and said, "I suppose I can go down there and have a look around."

"No suppose about it. You're going." Vail handed the report and a photograph across the desk to Longarm. The photograph was mounted on a thick, heavy piece of pasteboard with an oval cut out of it. "That's Matthew Chadwick."

5

Longarm briefly studied the young man's picture. Chadwick looked to be in his early to middle twenties, an earnest but handsome hombre with thick dark hair, mutton-chop sideburns, and a clean-shaven, cleft chin. In the picture he was posed sitting down, wearing an expensive suit with a bowler hat placed on his lap.

Longarm tossed the photograph back on Vail's desk, folded the report, and placed it in his coat pocket. "I'll know him if I see him," he said. "I don't need to carry around that picture."

"That's fine." Vail's voice softened just slightly. "I appreciate this, Custis. I know it's not the sort of thing we normally do around here. . . ."

"We investigate whatever the bosses in Washington tell us to investigate," said Longarm. "One case is as good as another."

But in his heart he knew that wasn't true. Some cases were a lot worse than others. There was no getting around that fact.

And his gut told him there was a better-than-even chance this might be one of the bad ones.

Longarm picked up his travel vouchers from Henry, the four-eyed young gent who played the typewriter in Vail's outer office. Then he packed a bag in his rented room on the other side of Cherry Creek and left Denver on the train.

He took the Union Pacific to Kansas City, where he made connections with a southbound Atchison, Topeka & Santa Fe train that took him down to Houston, Texas. From there he caught a Southern Pacific train that chugged across the marshy lowlands of southern Louisiana toward New Orleans.

In its entirety the trip took a couple of days and was un-eventful. He had spent an hour at the depot in Houston waiting for the eastbound train, and his shirt was wilted with sweat from the humidity by the end of that time. The stopover gave him a chance to study a railroad map he borrowed from the stationmaster, so he knew where to leave the train. It was a small town west of Baton Rouge. A road ran from there down to Saint Angelique.

After claiming his saddlebag, Winchester, and McClellan saddle, Longarm asked a clerk in the depot where he might be able to rent a horse. "You jus' go on down the street to Meriwether's Livery an' blacksmith shop. Meriwether, he got some horses an' he'll rent you one of 'em, I expect."

"Much obliged," said Longarm with a tug on the brim of his flat-crowned, snuff-brown Stetson. He left the station and followed the clerk's directions, as well as the ringing sound of a hammer striking an anvil.

When he stepped into the blacksmith shop next to the livery barn, he wasn't sure at first if it was a man wielding the hammer or a bear wearing a heavy leather apron. From behind, it could have been either one.

"Howdy," Longarm said when the smith raised the hammer to strike another blow on the horseshoe he was fashioning. Before turning around, the smith walloped the iron shoe again, but that must have put the finishing touches on it because he picked it up with a pair of tongs and dropped it in a bucket of water to cool.

Then he turned to face his visitor, and Longarm saw that the smith was indeed a man, one with massive shoulders and a pelt of coarse dark hair that would do justice to a grizzly. He was naked from the waist up except for the apron.

"Somethin' I can do you for, mister?" the smith rumbled through a tangled beard.

"If you're Mr. Meriwether, I'm looking to rent a horse," said Longarm.

"I'm Meriwether Dupree. C'mon next door to the corral. I'll show you what I got."

Three horses were in the corral behind the barn. Long-

7

arm thought all of them looked like decent animals. He settled on a big bay gelding, because Longarm wasn't a small
man and needed a sturdy horse to carry him.

Knowing that Henry had a tendency of questioning
everything he possibly could on expense accounts, Longarm negotiated what he thought was a fair price. Dupree
said, "Only reason I can go that low is 'cause you got your
own saddle and I don't have to throw in so much tack."

Longarm gestured toward the road that ran in front of
the place and asked, "Is this the trail that goes to Saint
Angelique?"

"Sure is. That where you're headed, Mr. . . . ?"

"Long. Custis Long." Longarm didn't add that he was a
deputy United States marshal. He was close enough now to
the area where Matthew Chadwick had vanished that it was
possible he might run into somebody who'd had something
to do with the young man's disappearance—assuming, of
course, that foul play was even involved. It was just as
likely that Chadwick simply had some sort of accident out
in the swamp, probably a fatal one.

"Must be goin' to Saint Angelique on business," said
Dupree.

"What makes you think that?"

The blacksmith grunted. "Ain't very likely anybody
would go there for pleasure. Not much down yonder in
Terrenoire Parish 'cept for swamps and a few plantations
and Saint Angelique. It's the parish seat."

Longarm didn't offer any explanation of why he was
going there, and Dupree didn't press him for one. Instead
the big lawman asked, "Friendly folks down thataway, are
they?"

"Friendly?" Dupree frowned under a shaggy thatch of
black hair. "Not so's you'd notice, I'd say. But I reckon
they're no better or worse than most folks when it comes to
that."

Longarm saddled the bay himself, slid the Winchester

8

into the attached sheath, and lashed the saddlebag on behind. Before he swung up, he paid Dupree what he owed.

"How long you goin' to be gone?" the blacksmith asked.

"Don't really know," replied Longarm. "Depends on how long it takes me to do my job."

Again, Dupree didn't ask what that job was. Longarm mounted up, clucked to the horse, and heeled the animal into a walk that carried horse and rider down the road at an easy pace.

"You be careful down yonder!" Dupree called after him, and in the smith's voice Longarm heard something that set his nerves on edge for a moment.

It sounded like Dupree didn't really expect him to come back from Saint Angelique.

That didn't make any sense, Longarm told himself. The man wouldn't have rented the horse to him if he didn't expect him to return.

Once they were out of town Longarm urged the horse into a faster gait. According to the map he had looked at, Saint Angelique was about twenty miles away. The hour was still early enough that he thought he could reach the settlement before nightfall.

He hoped so, anyway. From the looks of this road, it would be a dark, lonesome trail once the sun went down.

Big trees that dripped with Spanish moss crowded up to the road on both sides. They grew thickly along here, and the moss made them seem even more dense and foreboding. Occasionally the trees cleared and the sides of the road sloped down to show that it had been built up along those stretches. Thick grass grew in those open areas, and when Longarm looked more closely he saw the sun shining on water. The grass was growing out of a marsh.

In some places wildflowers clustered in such profusion that their perfume turned the air sickly sweet. An incessant cloud of mosquitoes buzzed around Longarm's head, and he saw a few beaver and muskrats and possums. Once he spotted a couple of what were apparently wild hogs on a hummock across a marsh. He was glad the feral beasts didn't try to come after him. Few things in the world were meaner than a wild hog.

He didn't see any wagons or other riders on the road, which was a little surprising. According to Meriwether Dupree, several plantations were located down here. It wouldn't have been uncommon to see people coming and going from them.

By the time Longarm thought he should be nearing Saint Angelique, the sun had dipped low in the western sky, and shadows were thick under the trees. Longarm knew that once the sun had set, darkness would close in quickly. But he had come this far and there was nothing he could do except keep going.

He reined in sharply, though, as he heard a sudden screech from somewhere nearby. It came from a cat of some kind, Longarm decided, probably a bobcat. The screech hadn't really sounded like the cry of a panther.

A bobcat could be dangerous, too. Longarm was reaching for his Winchester when instinct made him glance over his shoulder.

In the cloaking dimness, he saw a flicker of movement behind him. It was there for just an instant, and then whoever or whatever caused it disappeared into the trees at the side of the road. Even though the light was bad, Longarm thought the briefly glimpsed figure had belonged to a man.

And he would have sworn that the man was limping.

Chapter 2

Longarm went ahead and pulled the Winchester from its sheath, but he didn't see any further sign of the limping man, and the bobcat didn't screech again.

"You're getting jumpy, old son," he told himself aloud. "Just because some fella's walking through the woods don't mean it has anything to do with you."

The gloomy surroundings were getting to him, he decided.

But despite that he rode with the rifle across the saddle in front of him as he pushed on toward Saint Angelique.

The sun was down, but its afterglow remained in the sky when he reached the settlement. The lights that came from the windows of the building were welcome sights. The road became a wide, unpaved street that ran between several blocks of business buildings to a square where the parish courthouse was located.

Longarm knew that Louisiana was the only state with parishes rather than counties, but it was pretty much the same thing. He found a squat building fronting the town square with a sign over its door that read SHERIFF— TERRENOIRE PARISH. He dismounted, looped the bay's reins

11

around the hitch rack, and stepped onto the porch of the sheriff's office.

At that same moment, the office door swung open and a man stepped out. He and Longarm both stopped short. Jerking a thumb over his shoulder, the man said, "You got business with the sheriff, friend?"

"That's right," said Longarm. "Would you happen to be him?"

"I am. Name of Remy Duquesne. I was about to go get me some supper, but I 'spose it can wait." The sheriff laughed and slapped a hand against the ample belly that bulged over his belt. "Come on in."

Duquesne was tall, only a few inches shorter than Longarm, and big all over, from his shoulders to his belly to his legs, with thighs like tree trunks. Longarm had a feeling that despite being fat, Duquesne wasn't necessarily soft. When he took off his hat he revealed a full head of wavy brown hair. He nodded Longarm into a chair in front of the desk and settled down behind it in a chair that creaked under his weight. If he had any deputies, they weren't in the office at the moment.

"What can I do for you?"

Longarm reached into his coat and took out the leather folder that contained his badge and bona fides. Leaving it closed, he passed it across the desk to Duquesne. The sheriff took it, opened it, and studied what was inside with keen dark eyes set in deep pits of fat and gristle.

After a moment Duquesne snapped the folder closed and said, "Federal lawman, eh?" He handed the folder back to Longarm. "You must be in Saint Angelique on business."

Longarm didn't add that he'd already been told nobody would come here for pleasure. Duquesne might feel some loyalty to the town and take offense at the comment. Instead Longarm said, "I'm looking for somebody."

"A federal fugitive?"

"No, as far as I know this fella hasn't committed any crime. All he's done is gotten himself missing. His name is Matthew Chadwick."

Duquesne frowned and pursed his lips as he mulled over the name. After a moment he said, "Don't reckon I know him. I don't recall ever hearing the name."

"You've heard the name Chadwick, though, I expect. As in Senator Chadwick."

Duquesne drew in a deep breath and sat up straighter in his chair. It creaked under him again. "This fella you're looking for is related to the senator?"

"His son," said Longarm with a nod. "The report we got said that he was last seen around here and that he was heading into the swamp to search for Jean Lafitte's treasure."

Duquesne snorted in disgust. "Pirate loot! That old rumor!"

"You've heard about it before, then?" asked Longarm as he leaned forward a little.

Duquesne waved a hand with stubby fingers like sausages and said, "Hell, most folks around here have heard those old stories all their lives. Lafitte had a place down south of here on Barataria Bay, a regular little town where he and his men would come back after their raids out into the gulf. It's not too far, and you could pole up here in pirogues without any trouble. I guess somebody decided one day to claim that Lafitte hid some of his treasure in these parts, but I've lived here, man and boy, for more than forty years and I never seen any sign of no pirate gold."

"But do you remember a young man coming here who said he was going to look for it?"

Duquesne clasped his hands together over his belly. "Yeah, I remember him. His name wasn't Chadwick, though. He called himself something else. Chamberlain, seems like, or Charleston. Yeah, that was it, Charleston, like the town in South Carolina."

So Matthew Chadwick had concealed his real identity

13

from the people of Saint Angelique. Longarm wasn't sure why he would have done such a thing. Maybe it had to do with that old diary he was supposed to have found. Maybe he just didn't want to draw any attention to himself.

In that case he shouldn't have announced that he was going to hunt for pirate treasure in the swamp. "You think somebody could have followed him and tried to rob him?" asked Longarm.

"Anything's possible. Most folks around here are pretty much law-abiding, though."

"You didn't notice that Chadwick left town and didn't come back?"

"It's not my job to keep up with strangers who are foolish enough to wander off into the swamp," Duquesne said. His voice held impatience and irritation now. "For all I know, he could have left the swamp and gone on somewhere else."

"Or maybe a gator got him," suggested Longarm.

Duquesne gave an emphatic nod. "Or maybe a gator got him, that's right. It's sure been known to happen."

"Is there any chance he hired a guide, somebody who could have gone into the swamp with him?"

"I wouldn't know. Feel free to ask around town. Some of the old-timers around here probably would have been willing to hire on with him. These old boys will do just about anything for money as long as it's not too hard."

Longarm nodded. "All right. Is there anything else you can tell me, Sheriff?"

"Not a blessed thing except that there's a big plate of red beans and rice waiting for me over at the café, and I intend to go eat it." Duquesne put his hands flat on his desk and pushed himself to his feet with a grunt of effort. "You can tell me something, though, Marshal."

"What's that?"

"Why in hell does the federal government waste money

14

sending somebody down here to look for a boy who was too dumb to stay out of the swamp?"

"Because that boy's pa is a United States senator."

Duquesne grunted again. His initial attitude of affability had completely vanished by now. He put on his hat and said, "If you'll excuse me, Marshal . . ."

Longarm went to the door and paused to look over his shoulder. "You don't mind if I poke around some?"

"Help yourself. Just don't bother me anymore with this fool's errand."

Longarm felt his temper flare. He didn't like being called a fool, even by implication. But he reined in his anger and gave Duquesne a curt nod as he went out. He had planned to ask the sheriff where the best place was to stay in Saint Angelique, but he didn't feel like talking to the local lawman anymore.

Instead he untied his horse and walked along the street until he came to a livery stable. A wizened old black man was working there, and as he took the bay he said in reply to Longarm's question, "Only one real hotel in town. That be the Giddings House. Go one more block, and it'll be on your left."

"I'm obliged," said Longarm. He flipped a coin to the old-timer and was about to turn away, but then he stopped and asked, "Do you recall renting a horse to a young fella who was planning to go out in the swamp? Would have been about a month ago, more than likely."

The old man shook his head and said solemnly, "I wouldn't rent no horse to a man like that. He'd jus' go and get that poor hoss et up by a gator, an' his own self, too."

Longarm nodded. Matthew Chadwick might have already had a horse when he reached Saint Angelique, but the question had been worth asking.

He ventured another. "Do you know anybody around here who's got a bad limp?"

The old man's eyes widened a little, but he shook his head and said without hesitation, "No, sir, I sure don't. Don't know nobody like that at all."

He was lying. Longarm was sure of that. His years of experience as a lawman had given him a fairly reliable instinct for the truth, and the old liveryman wasn't telling it.

But the look in the old man's eyes when Longarm mentioned a limping man had been one of fear, so Longarm just nodded as if he accepted the answer. He wasn't sure why he had asked the question in the first place; the man he had seen out on the road—if indeed he had even seen such a man—didn't have anything to do with the job that had brought him here.

The old-timer's reaction was intriguing, though. Maybe he would ask around some more about the limping man, Longarm told himself.

Just to satisfy his curiosity.

He got a room at the Giddings House and left his bag and Winchester there. The hotel had a dining room, so he went there to eat instead of venturing out in search of a café or hash house. He didn't much want to run into Sheriff Remy Duquesne again. Just because he'd managed to hold his temper once didn't mean he could do it again.

The hotel didn't seem to have many guests. The lobby hadn't been crowded, and neither was the dining room. Longarm ordered a bowl of gumbo. It came with a big hunk of freshly baked bread to help soak up some of the fiery spices. He was about halfway through the bowl when a woman came in and sat down at one of the other tables.

She drew his eye because she was young and pretty. Somewhere between twenty and twenty-five, he judged. The hair pinned up under a stylish little hat was ash blond, and her eyes were dark blue. She looked over at Longarm and met his gaze levelly. She didn't look unfriendly, but she wasn't overly encouraging, either.

She wasn't wearing a wedding ring, he noted.

He hadn't come all the way down here to Louisiana to look at women, no matter how pretty they were, so he turned his attention back to his meal. When the waiter brought coffee, Longarm asked him, "You know anybody around here who hires out to guide folks into the swamps?"

The man frowned in thought, then said, "You might ask Pierre Jacquard. He's lived all his life 'round here. I think he sometimes hires out to gents from Baton Rouge and N'Orleans when they come down here to hunt and fish."

"Where do I find him?"

"He's got a shack on the edge of town. Go up to the last cross street, turn left, and then Jacquard's place will be the last one on the right."

"Much obliged." Longarm nodded.

"You aim to do some of that, mister? Huntin' or fishin', I mean."

"Hunting," said Longarm.

He lingered over his coffee. The young woman he had noticed earlier didn't eat much and left the dining room first, even though she had come in after he did. When Longarm walked from the hotel dining room into the lobby, he paused to debate with himself what he should do next—go see Pierre Jacquard or turn in for the night, figuring that that morning would be soon enough to talk to Jacquard.

He decided to see if he could find Jacquard. The sooner he determined what had happened to Matthew Chadwick, the sooner he could leave Louisiana and get back to Denver.

As he left the hotel, he lit a cheroot. Trailing clouds of smoke, he walked along the street and followed the waiter's directions. Most of the buildings were dark now. The citizens of Saint Angelique retired early.

Light shone through the oilcloth that covered the windows of Pierre Jacquard's home. It was a ramshackle wooden building that leaned slightly and wasn't big enough to contain more than two rooms. Maybe just one. Longarm stepped up onto the porch and felt the boards sag a little under his weight. He hoped they wouldn't collapse.

A line of light showed at the gap between the closed door and the jamb. He was about to knock when the door was suddenly jerked open. Light spilled out around him. Somebody rushed from the shack in a hurry and ran right into him. The softness of the body that collided with his, plus the high-pitched little cry, told him that the person leaving the shack so hastily was a woman.

But he wasn't expecting to see the fair-haired beauty he had noticed in the hotel dining room only a short time earlier.

He put a hand on her arm to steady her. "Hold on there, ma'am," he said. "What's the rush?"

"Let me go," she said, a note of desperation in her voice. "You've got to let me go."

"I just want to make sure you're all right. You ran into me pretty hard—"

"If I hurt you, I apologize."

Longarm made an effort not to chuckle. A little bitty thing like her could run into him all day without hurting him. It was *she* who had bounced off *him*, not the other way around.

"Don't worry, I'm fine," he told her. Suspicion was alive in him. "You had business with the fella who lives here? Pierre Jacquard?"

"I . . . I don't know him. I never saw him before!" Desperation was rapidly turning into hysteria. "Please, I must go."

Longarm's hand tightened on her arm. Something was wrong here, and he didn't particularly need a lawman's instincts to see that. He looked past her. . . .

And saw a man's booted foot lying on the floor next to a rickety old table.

"Let's step back inside," said Longarm. He had caught a

18

whiff of something that smelled like shaved copper. His voice was harder now, with a sound that said he wouldn't accept any argument.

She tried to give him one anyway. As she struggled to pull loose from his grip, she said, "No, I have to go. I didn't have anything to do with it, I swear! I found him that way! He was like that when I got here!"

Longarm stepped into the shack, forcing the young woman to come with him. She gave a choked gasp and turned her head away so that she wouldn't have to look at what was lying on the floor beside the table.

The man was mostly bald, with a tuft of chin whiskers like a billy goat. Those whiskers had been white, but they were stained red now from the blood that had splashed up on them when somebody slashed the man's throat. The cut was deep, and it stretched from one side of the neck to the other. A pool of dark crimson had formed around the man's head and shoulders and was still spreading slowly. He hadn't been dead for long.

But he was dead, sure enough. Longarm didn't have a doubt in hell about that.

Nor did he doubt that he was looking at the mortal remains of Pierre Jacquard.

"You say he was like this when you found him?" asked Longarm in that hard voice.

Still unwilling to look at the corpse, the young woman jerked her head in a nod.

"You didn't see who did it?"

She shook her head.

"When you came up, did you notice anybody nearby, like they might've just left here?"

"I . . . I'm not sure. It's so dark. But I thought I saw a man hurry around the building and head for the trees. . . ."

Instinct prompted the next question that came from Longarm. "Did he have a limp?"

"N-now that you mention it, I . . . I think he did."

Longarm nodded grimly. He didn't know what that answer meant, but he wasn't surprised by it.

"What are we going to do?" asked the young woman.

"I reckon we'd better go tell the sheriff what happened."

"Do we have to?"

"I don't see any getting around it."

Longarm still had hold of her arm. He turned her toward the door. He wanted to take a look around the inside of the shack to see if Jacquard had anything that might link him to Matthew Chadwick, but Longarm preferred to do that while the young woman wasn't here. As they stepped out onto the porch, he decided he would tell her to go to the sheriff's office to report the killing while he stayed here to guard the body. That would give him a chance to search the place.

He might have done that if just then a gun hadn't roared and sent a bullet whistling past his ear.

Chapter 3

Colt flame had bloomed in the darkness to Longarm's right. He went to his left, the side that the young woman was on. Once again they collided. This time Longarm drove her all the way off the porch. He went with her. Both of them sprawled on the ground.

More shots blasted. Slugs chewed splinters from the boards of the porch. But it was elevated enough so that it provided some cover for Longarm and the woman. Staying low, he grabbed her and rolled behind the corner of the shack.

"Stay here and keep your head down," he told her as he reached across his body and pulled the Colt from the cross-draw rig on his left hip. He came up on one knee and eased himself past the corner of the shack just far enough to squeeze off a couple of shots. He aimed at the spot where he had seen the muzzle flashes a moment earlier.

The bushwhacker was already on the move and returned Longarm's fire from a location to the left of where he had been. Longarm ducked back as bullets sizzled through the air near his head.

Lamps were being lit in other houses along the road as the shots roused people from sleep. A door banged open, and a man yelled, "Hey! What the hell's goin' on out there?"

Longarm didn't answer and neither did the would-be killer. Crouching, Longarm moved back until he reached the young woman, who lay there with her face pressed hard to the ground. She was obviously terrified, and he couldn't blame her. First she had found a man with his head halfway cut off, and then somebody had tried to kill her. He reached down, grasped her arm, and pulled her to her feet.

"Come on," he said. "We're getting out of here."

"I thought we were going to tell the sheriff—"

"That can wait," he cut in. The ambush had changed things. Now he wanted some answers before he talked to Remy Duquesne again. Longarm ran with the woman into the trees that grew fairly close to the rear of the shack. The shadows were so thick that they had to slow down and feel their way along.

More shouts prompted Longarm to look back toward the shack. Through some narrow gaps in the trees he saw Sheriff Duquesne trotting ponderously along the road. A lantern swayed in his left hand. In his right Duquesne held a shotgun. He had heard the shots, too, and had come to investigate.

"Keep moving," Longarm whispered to the woman.

She balked. "Why? Why can't we just tell the sheriff what happened?"

"Because he might not believe us," said Longarm. "He might think that *you* cut Jacquard's throat."

The woman gasped. "What? That's insane! I wouldn't have hurt him. I was going to him for help."

"Yeah, I want to hear about that," muttered Longarm. He recalled that the woman had been sitting near enough to him in the hotel dining room that she could have overheard his conversation with the waiter. She had heard the man tell Longarm that Pierre Jacquard might hire out as a guide into the swamp, and she had left pretty soon after the waiter had told him how to find Jacquard's shack.

Clearly, she had wanted to get to Jacquard before Longarm had a chance to. And he wanted to know why.

He asked himself if it was possible that she had actually killed Jacquard, rather than finding him already murdered. She would have had to be a pretty good actress to carry off that deception, but he decided that he couldn't rule it out. That made him even more eager to find out what her connection was to Jacquard.

Then there was the matter of the limping man . . .

Longarm gave a little shake of his head as he made his way carefully through the thick growth. One mystery at a time, he told himself.

They left the trees, walked through an alley, and came out on the main street. Longarm thought they were far enough away from Jacquard's shack so that no one would connect them with the murdered man. In the glow from a nearby lighted window he looked down at himself and the young woman and saw that their clothes were disheveled, a little muddy in places, and had leaves clinging to them.

"Best brush yourself off," he advised her. "Otherwise when we go back into the hotel folks might notice that we've been rolling around on the ground."

"I certainly wouldn't want them to think that," she replied in a cold, angry voice. "How would *that* look?"

Longarm picked leaves off his trousers and coat. "It wasn't my idea to have somebody try to bushwhack us," he pointed out. "I figured you'd rather get knocked down than shot."

"They were shooting at *you*."

He grunted. "Know that for a fact, do you? How come they couldn't have been shooting at you?"

"No one has any reason to try to kill me."

23

"You found that fella with his throat cut. Maybe the bushwhacker didn't want you going to the sheriff and reporting the murder."

She looked up sharply from trying to put her clothes back in order. "You think whoever shot at us was the same one who killed that poor old man?"

"No way of knowing for sure," said Longarm with a shrug, "but it stands to reason. The hombre wanted Jacquard dead, and he wanted to kill anybody who came looking for the old man, too."

"But why?"

"You tell me."

"First tell me who you are," she said.

"My name is Custis Long."

"You're not from Louisiana, are you? You don't sound like the people who live around here."

"No, ma'am. I was born in West-by-God Virginia, but I've spent most of the last fifteen years or so in the West." He didn't add that he had spent much of that time as a federal lawman.

"What was *your* business with Mr. Jacquard? As they say, turnabout is fair play."

There was nothing fair or playful about murder, thought Longarm. He said, "I reckon you're right. We both need to put our cards on the table. But not here."

"Where, then?"

"Let's go back to the hotel," he suggested. "You're staying there, too, aren't you?"

She hesitated but then nodded. "How did you know I don't live around here?"

"You may not be as far from your usual stompin' grounds as I am, but a lady like you doesn't belong in this little backwater parish, either. If I had to guess I'd say you're from a bigger place. Baton Rouge, maybe, or even New Orleans."

24

"I do live in New Orleans," she admitted. "Just north of there, across the lake, actually."

Longarm nodded and offered her his arm. He had brushed himself off as best he could, and so had she. Again she hesitated, then slipped her arm through his. As they headed down the street toward the Giddings House, they looked like a couple out for an evening stroll. None of the few people on the street seemed to be paying any attention to them.

But appearances could be deceptive, Longarm reminded himself. Whoever had taken those shots at them could be watching right now.

Before they went inside the hotel, the woman said, "We'll talk in the lobby. I can't go to your room, and you can't come to mine. It wouldn't be proper."

Longarm had never given much of a hoot about propriety, but he didn't force the issue. He said, "As long as we find a place where nobody can eavesdrop on us, that'll be fine."

The lobby was deserted except for the clerk drowsing behind the desk. He roused briefly when Longarm and the woman came in, but when he saw that they were guests who had already registered, he went back to his half doze. Longarm escorted the woman to a couple of armchairs in a far corner of the lobby, next to a potted palm that was starting to wilt a little.

When they were seated, regarding each other warily, Longarm said, "I told you my name. I reckon it's time you told me yours."

"I'm Natalie Stoneham," she said.

The name didn't mean anything to Longarm. He said, "Why'd you go to Jacquard's shack?"

"I heard what you asked the waiter and what he told you. I need someone to guide me into the swamp, so I thought that I should go see this Mr. Jacquard first and try to engage his services. I was afraid that if I waited you would have already hired him."

That made sense—sort of. In a voice he was careful to keep pitched quietly enough so that it wouldn't be overheard, he asked Natalie Stoneham, "Why in the world does a woman like you want to go into the swamp?"

"I don't think that's any of your business, Mr. Long."

"Well, ask yourself this," he said. "Could the reason you wanted to hire Jacquard have anything to do with him being killed?"

Her face was already pale, but it grew even more so as she thought about what he had just said. After a moment she shook her head and said, "That's impossible. I . . . I'm just looking for someone. . . ."

"In the swamp?" Longarm took a guess. "Matthew Chadwick?"

Natalie's eyes widened. "How do you know that name? How do you know he's missing?"

"Because I'm looking for him, too."

Longarm hoped he wasn't making a mistake by telling her why he had come to Saint Angelique. He leaned toward believing that she hadn't killed Jacquard. His gut told him that whoever had taken those potshots at the two of them was responsible for that crime.

But Natalie was still mixed up in this, too, right up to her pretty little neck.

"What's your connection to Chadwick? He your beau?"

"Good Lord, no. He's my cousin. We practically grew up together. We're more like brother and sister than cousins."

"Then his pa the senator is—"

"My mother's brother, yes," Natalie said. "My uncle Tobias."

Longarm nodded, but he was still a little skeptical. With a slight frown, he said, "So when you heard that your cousin was missing, you just dropped everything and came down here to look for him?"

Her chin lifted in a defiant tilt. "You can believe it or not, Mr. Long, but it happens to be true. Now . . . I've put my cards on the table, as you phrased it, so it's time for you to do the same. Why are you here, and what do you know about Matthew's disappearance? You're obviously well-informed."

"I'm a deputy United States marshal. At your uncle's request, I was sent down here to find your cousin . . . or find out what happened to him."

Her lips tightened. "You think he's dead?"

"When a fella disappears in the swamp, the chances of good news are pretty slim," Longarm said. "There are a lot of things out there, and most of 'em are bad."

Natalie closed her eyes for a moment, then opened them and nodded as she said, "I've been afraid of that myself. But I can't bring myself to give up hope, Mr. Long. Or should I say Marshal Long?"

"Why don't you just make it Custis?" he suggested. "Since we're putting our cards on the table and all. And there's nothing wrong with hope. Hang on to it for as long as you can."

They sat there in silence for a moment, both thinking about what they had just learned. Finally Natalie said, "What about the man I thought I saw, the one with the limp? Was he the one who killed Mr. Jacquard?"

"I don't know," said Longarm with a shake of his head. "I thought I saw a fella with a limp earlier today, out on the trail while I was riding down here."

"Someone who was following you?" she asked with a quick interest.

"No, he was on foot. He couldn't have been following me. He was already in these parts before I got here."

"Then he might have had something to do with Matthew's disappearance."

"Maybe." Longarm frowned in thought as he rasped a thumbnail along the line of his jaw, then tugged on the lobe of his right ear. "The only reason we have to think that is because you might have seen him at Jacquard's shack. But earlier this evening I asked the fella at the livery stable if he knew of a limping man around here, and his answer made me a mite suspicious."

"What was it?"

"He claimed he didn't know of anybody like that," said Longarm, "but he looked scared when he said it, like he didn't want to admit that he knew who I was talking about."

"You should go ask him again, and make him tell you the truth this time. You're an officer of the law."

"Yeah, but that don't mean I want to start bullying an old man." Longarm put his hands on his knees and pushed himself to his feet. "Stay here. I'll go see if the desk clerk can tell me anything."

Natalie looked like she didn't care much for being told to stay put, but she didn't argue. Longarm went over to the desk. The clerk was all the way asleep now, with his chair tipped back against the wall.

Longarm rapped sharply on the desk. The clerk jumped and sat up. The legs of the chair thumped on the floor. His mouth opened and closed for a few seconds like that of a fish before his senses returned to him. Blinking, he looked up at Longarm and said, "Oh, howdy, Mr. Long. What can I do for you?"

"I was just wondering," said Longarm, "if you know a fella around here who has a bad limp."

For the second time this evening, he saw the flash of fear in a man's eyes as he asked that question. The clerk was even worse at concealing it than the old-timer at the livery stable had been.

But despite that, the man said, "N-no, I don't reckon I do. Can't think of anybody like that around here, Mr. Long."

Frustration welled up inside Longarm. The possibility that the limping man might be connected to the case that brought him here made him want to reach across the desk, grab the clerk by his scrawny neck, and shake the truth out of him. Billy Vail probably wouldn't take kindly to that, though, if he ever found out about it.

Not that Longarm hadn't bent the rules before, on plenty of occasions.

He nodded and said, "All right, but if you think of anybody, I'd be obliged if you'd let me know."

"Of course, Mr. Long."

Longarm went back to the armchair in the corner and sat down next to Natalie Stoneham. "The fella says he doesn't know any limping man," he told her, "but he's lying."

"How do you know?"

"Because he looked like a snake had just crawled up his leg when I asked him. Whoever the fella with the limp is, he's got folks around here spooked. They're too scared to even talk about him."

"Then he must have something to do with Matthew's disappearance!"

"Not necessarily," Longarm said.

"But if he was at Mr. Jacquard's shack—"

"We don't know that your cousin hired Jacquard to take him into the swamp," Longarm reminded her. "That's just a guess at this point."

Natalie slumped back in her chair. Her shoulders sagged with disappointment and despair. "I don't believe that we've reached a dead end," she said. "I can't allow myself to believe that."

She was talking like the two of them were in this search together. She had gotten over her initial suspicions of him mighty quickly, he mused. But he had told her that he was a lawman, and maybe that made her trust him.

He said, "Do you know why Matthew was down here in the first place?"

Trust only went so far, especially where pirate treasure was concerned. Natalie said, "I'm not sure. Matthew was a great student of history, and I think he had some theory he wanted to investigate . . ."

If she knew anything about the diary, she wasn't going to reveal it. Longarm decided that he would play those cards close to the vest, too, if that was the way she wanted it.

The important thing now was to convince her that she needed to give up her search and go back to New Orleans where she would be safe. The ambush outside Jacquard's shack told Longarm that someone didn't want him in Saint Angelique. Although he couldn't prove yet that the attempt on his life had anything to do with Matthew Chadwick's disappearance, it was an easy assumption to make. Having Natalie around would just complicate his investigation and probably put her in danger.

Even though he had just met her, he expected her to argue when he told her that she couldn't stay. She had to be pretty headstrong to have come down here on her own like this to look for her cousin.

Before he could say anything about what he wanted her to do, the front door of the hotel opened and Sheriff Remy Duquesne came in. He still carried the shotgun, but he didn't have the lantern anymore. He glanced around the lobby, and as his gaze fell on Longarm and Natalie, a dark frown creased his forehead. He started across the lobby toward them.

"Marshal Long!" he said in a loud, angry voice. "I want to talk to you about the murder of Pierre Jacquard!"

Chapter 4

Longarm came to his feet and returned Duquesne's glare with a cool stare of his own. The sheriff's words were confirmation of the dead man's identity, although Longarm had had no real doubt that he was Pierre Jacquard.

Longarm glanced at Natalie and hoped that she would follow his lead, then said, "I'm afraid I don't know what you're talking about, Sheriff."

"I'm talking about Pierre Jacquard laying down there in his shack with his throat cut!"

Longarm shook his head. "I'm afraid I don't know a thing about it."

"But you know who Jacquard was?"

Duquesne wouldn't have connected him with Jacquard unless he already knew what the waiter had told Longarm in the dining room. Otherwise he wouldn't have had any reason to think that Longarm had been anywhere near Jacquard's shack tonight.

Realizing that, Longarm said, "I know Jacquard was an old-timer who was familiar with the swamps around here. Fella who works in the dining room told me that Jacquard might hire out as a guide from time to time."

"So you went to see him after you left here?" snapped Duquesne.

Longarm had been telling the truth up to this point, but now he shook his head. "No. I was going to, but I never made it down there. I ran into Miss Stoneham here"—he waved a hand toward Natalie—"and I've been talking to her instead."

The desk clerk would be able to confirm that Longarm and Natalie had been here in the hotel lobby for a while. Half asleep as the man had been, he probably didn't know for sure when they came in. He wouldn't be able to swear that Longarm and Natalie hadn't entered the hotel until after all the shooting over at Jacquard's place.

That was Longarm's hope, anyway.

Duquesne's piggish glare switched to Natalie for a second. He tugged on the brim of his hat and grunted, "Ma'am."

Longarm said, "Are you telling me this fella Jacquard got himself killed tonight?"

"Yeah. Got his throat cut. Not too long ago, by the looks of the blood."

Natalie shuddered convincingly. Longarm figured it wasn't an act. She had been very shaken up by the sight of the dead man.

"As one lawman to another, I wish I could help you, Sheriff," Longarm said. "It's too bad I didn't go on down to see Jacquard like I planned to. I might have caught the killer or even been able to save his life."

"Yeah, it's a damned shame." Duquesne didn't sound too convinced of that. "You sure you didn't see anything?"

"Not a thing," said Longarm with a shake of his head.

"All right, then." The sheriff tucked the shotgun under his arm. "I guess I'll go back down there and take a better look around. Killer might've dropped something that'd put me on his trail."

"Good luck," said Longarm. He wasn't sure if he meant it or not. He was leaning toward "not."

Duquesne left the hotel. Longarm extended a hand to Natalie and said, "I'll escort you up to your room, Miss Stoneham."

She took his hand and stood up. "Are we through talking, then?" she asked quietly.

"Play along with me," Longarm told her, equally quietly.

Arm in arm, they crossed the lobby to the stairs. As they passed the desk, Longarm nodded to the clerk.

When they were halfway up the stairs, Natalie said, "That man is probably thinking scandalous things, what with the two of us going up together."

"Let him think what he wants. We're not done yet, but I want some privacy before we continue with this."

"I told you, Marshal Long, we can't be alone in the same room."

"I reckon I can control myself if you can," growled Longarm.

Natalie reddened and sputtered a little, but then she broke into an unexpected grin. "Oh, all right," she said, "but I'll hold you to that."

They went to her room, which was across the hall and several doors down from Longarm's. As they passed his door he glanced down and saw a small piece of a matchstick lying on the floor in front of it, near the jamb.

Natalie must have felt him stiffen. "What's wrong?" she asked.

He didn't answer her question directly. Instead he said, "The sheriff didn't seem to know you. You didn't go to see him and ask him about your cousin when you got into town?"

She shook her head. "No, I hadn't gotten around to it yet. I just arrived earlier today, and I was worn out from the trip."

"You're probably lucky you were tired. But just in case. . . . give me your key and let me go in first." He reached for his gun as he said it.

Natalie's eyebrows arched. "Are you sure that's necessary?"

"Nope. But I'd just as soon not take a chance."

She opened her bag and brought out the key to her room. As she handed it over to him, Longarm drew his Colt.

"Stay here."

She nodded. A frightened look was on her face again.

Moving carefully and quietly, he went to the door of her room. The key was in his left hand, the revolver in his right. He thrust the key into the lock and turned it, and at the same time he took a swift step to the right, just in case someone inside the room had been listening for the rasp of the key and was ready to fire through the door.

Nothing happened.

Still standing to one side of the door, Longarm reached over, grasped the knob, turned it. He pushed the door open. The room inside was dark. He went in fast, crouching low and pivoting from side to side, the gun in his fist ready to spout flame and death.

In the light from the hallway, he saw that the room was empty except for the few items of furniture.

When he stepped back out into the hall, Natalie asked in an anxious voice, "Is everything all right?"

"Yeah, there's nobody there. But there could've been, and I'd rather feel a mite foolish than a whole heap dead."

He holstered the Colt and motioned for her to join him. As she came into the room he snapped a match to life and held the flame to the wick of the lamp on a small bedside table. When he lowered the chimney, the warm yellow glow spread out and filled the room. The curtains were drawn over the window, and Longarm pulled the shade down, too, as Natalie closed the door. He didn't want that bushwhacker to take another shot at them, through the window this time.

There was only one chair in the room, so Natalie sat on the bed. Longarm took the ladderback chair, turned it around, and straddled it.

As she unpinned her hat from the upswept mass of her hair, Natalie asked, "What was that all about, Marshal Long? Did you have reason to suspect that someone might be lurking in here?"

"Not really. I reckon whoever was skulking around up here earlier was content to search my room."

She frowned at him. "How do you know someone was in your room?"

"I'm in the habit of putting a little piece of matchstick between the door and the jamb when I close the door," he explained. "When the door is opened, that matchstick falls out, but it's small enough that whoever goes into the room usually doesn't notice it."

"I see. And the matchstick was dislodged when we came upstairs?"

"That's right. I figure Sheriff Duquesne had himself a look around my room while I was downstairs at dinner."

She stared at him. "Sheriff Duquesne? But he's an officer of the law. Why would he do such a thing?"

"Maybe because he *is* a lawman and he doesn't trust me. Or maybe he's got some other reason we don't know about yet."

"How do you know it was him?"

"The only people I talked to in town were Duquesne, the waiter, the desk clerk, and an old man who works at the livery stable. The waiter I only asked about a hunting guide, and the old-timer didn't have any reason to be sneaking around in my room."

"The clerk could have been looking for something to steal," suggested Natalie.

35

"Maybe, but even petty thievery seems like a pretty ambitious crime for a fella who can hardly stay awake."

"That could be a pose."

Longarm shrugged. "Could be. But Duquesne knows who I am and he knew why I came to Saint Angelique, because I stopped and told him when I got into town. Professional courtesy, I reckon you could call it. He claimed then that he didn't know anything about your cousin. He remembered him and knew he was missing, but he didn't know who Matthew really was. Said that Matthew was going by the name Charleston instead of Chadwick."

"I'm not surprised," Natalie said. "When Matthew was a young man, he became very stubborn about not trading on his father's famous name. Whatever he did, he wanted to succeed in it through his own efforts, not because he was the son of a United States senator."

"Didn't like being in the old man's shadow, eh?"

"You could say that," admitted Natalie. "So using a false name sounds very much like something he would do."

That cleared up one mystery, anyway. Longarm went on, "Duquesne was mighty surprised when he found out who Matthew really was. I figure he searched my room to see if he could find out anything else he didn't already know."

"Why would he do that?"

Longarm put into words the theory that had been forming in his brain. "Because I think he might have something to do with your cousin's disappearance."

Natalie stared at him as if she couldn't quite comprehend what he had just told her. After a moment she said, "But he's the sheriff."

"I've run into plenty of star packers who were as crooked as a dog's hind leg. If Duquesne is mixed up with Matthew's disappearance, there's a good chance he'd want to cover up that fact. That would explain why he searched my room. He wants to know exactly how much *I* know.

He's mighty interested in what I do, too. He had already talked to that waiter and found out that I was asking about a guide into the swamp. He knew that I'd been told about Pierre Jacquard."

Natalie clasped her hands together, shook her head, and frowned. "This is getting too convoluted for me, Marshal Long . . . Custis. I just can't believe that a lawman would do such a thing."

"He may have done worse than just search a hotel room," said Longarm. "I'm not sure but he might have killed Jacquard."

"What!" The exclamation was startled out of Natalie.

Longarm took a deep breath. What he had to say to Natalie required some plain talk, and he hoped she was up to it.

"I think your cousin is probably dead. Could have been foul play. Say he hired Jacquard as a guide. Jacquard took him into the swamp, all right, but when he got him out there, he killed him and robbed him. But he had to split the loot with Duquesne, because the sheriff knew what Jacquard was up to. Duquesne might have even planned the whole thing. That was fine when Matthew Charleston was just some unimportant stranger. But then I rode in and told him that Charleston was really Matthew Chadwick, the son of Senator Tobias Chadwick. Not only that, but now a federal lawman was looking for him, too. Duquesne wouldn't have wanted me to talk to Jacquard because he thought that the old-timer might break down and confess. So while I was eating dinner, Duquesne searched my room and then hurried down to Jacquard's shack and cut his throat."

Natalie looked like she was struggling to keep up with the theory, but at least she wasn't completely discarding the idea. She wasn't completely sold on it, either, though.

"Does that mean Sheriff Duquesne was the one who shot at us when we left the shack?" she asked.

"Probably. He'd want to keep an eye on the place, just in case I came along after he killed Jacquard. You would have been a surprise to him, but once he saw you with me, you became a target, too."

Natalie shook her head. "But he came running to investigate the shooting," she objected. "We saw him through the trees with our own eyes."

"The shooting had stopped a few minutes before that," Longarm pointed out. "He had time to circle around, grab a lantern and a shotgun out of his office, and pretend that he was coming to see what was going on. Saint Angelique's not such a big place that he couldn't do that."

"I suppose so."

The facts were fitting together better in Longarm's mind as he laid them out, prompting him to revise his theory. "He knew that we were there, because he saw us. So he didn't even have to talk to the waiter. He figured that's who must have told me about Jacquard. But he didn't know who you are. He still doesn't know that you're Matthew's cousin."

"Then who does he think I am?" she asked.

Longarm grinned. "Some lady I picked up as companionship for the evening?"

She flushed. "That's terrible! Are you telling me that I look like a . . . a scarlet woman?"

"Take it easy," he told her. "That's better than him knowing who you really are. You'll be safer that way until you can get out of here and go back to New Orleans."

"What makes you think I'm going back to New Orleans?" she snapped.

That reaction was one of the things Longarm had been worried about. He said, "Look, Miss Stoneham . . . Natalie. All that I've been telling you about Sheriff Duquesne is just a theory. I can't prove any of it at this point. But here's something that ain't a theory. Pierre Jacquard is dead." He deliberately made his voice hard. "Somebody cut his head halfway off. And then somebody, more than likely the same person, tried to kill us, too. Whatever is going on here, it's mighty serious . . . and mighty dangerous."

"I can't just give up on finding Matthew."

"I'm not asking you to. I'm just saying you need to go back to New Orleans and let me find out what happened to him."

"But you think he's dead," she said in a half whisper that was taut with emotional strain. "I still hope he's alive."

"So do I."

"But you don't believe it."

"I'm not sure anybody would go to so much trouble to keep things covered up if he wasn't dead." Longarm hated to say it to her, but it was true.

Stubbornly, she shook her head. "I'm not leaving, Marshal. I know you want me out of the way so you won't have to be worrying about me, but I can't just give up." Once again her chin took on that defiant tilt. "For one thing, your theory isn't complete. It's missing something."

"What's that?" Longarm asked.

"Who is the limping man, and how is he involved in Matthew's disappearance?"

Longarm didn't have an answer for that. He frowned and said, "I've still got to ponder on that one. Like the old hymn says, farther along we'll know more about it."

"And I can help you find out the truth," insisted Natalie.

"It's late," said Longarm with a rueful shake of his head. "We'll talk about it some more in the morning." He pushed himself to his feet and turned the chair back the way it had been. "Until then, keep your door locked and don't open it to anybody except me. I don't reckon you've got a gun."

She shook her head.

He sighed and reached to the heavy silver watch chain that looped across his vest. On one end was attached the turnip watch that he had carried for years. It was a dependable timepiece.

The other end of the chain was welded to a small, over-and-under two-barrel .41-caliber derringer. The little gun rode in his other vest pocket like a deadly watch fob. It had saved his life more times than he liked to count. Now he removed watch, chain, and derringer and handed them to Natalie.

"It's loaded," he told her. "All you have to do is cock the hammer and pull the trigger. Cock it again to use the second barrel."

"I . . . I couldn't actually *shoot* somebody."

"You'd be surprised what you can do if somebody's trying to kill you," Longarm assured her. "Hang on to it, anyway, so I won't worry as much about you."

"Well . . . all right."

Longarm told her that he would see her first thing in the morning, and they would figure out then what to do next. What he still intended was to send her back to New Orleans—but he was sure that she was equally determined to stay in Saint Angelique until the mystery of her cousin's disappearance was solved.

He waited outside the door until he'd heard her turn the key in the lock. Then he went down the hall to his room. The displaced matchstick proved that the door had been opened, but it didn't say anything about whether or not the intruder was still inside. Although he doubted that anybody was lurking in there, Longarm went through the same routine of carefully unlocking the door and going in fast and low, ready for trouble.

No one was waiting for him, but he could tell that somebody had pawed through his bag. The fact that his belongings had been searched made him more convinced than ever that Sheriff Remy Duquesne was mixed up in this.

Longarm opened the window to let in some fresh air, stripped down to his long underwear, smoked a last cheroot while he thought over everything that had happened since his arrival in Saint Angelique, and then stretched out on the bed. He stared at the ceiling as sleep was slow in coming. Something Natalie had said was still nagging at him.

Just who the hell *was* that limping man, anyway?

Chapter 5

Longarm dozed off after a while, and even though his sleep was deep and dreamless, a part of him remained alert. That habit had been ingrained in him by years of survival in a dangerous profession.

So when a soft thump sounded in the room, followed by another and then another, he roused from slumber, aware that something was wrong even though he didn't know exactly what it was.

His eyes opened, but he lay there motionless and silent, giving no indication that he was awake as his senses searched the darkness for a hint of what had just happened.

The room was quiet. No floorboards creaked underfoot, and the curtains over the window didn't even move because the night breezes had died away to nothing. He asked himself if he had imagined whatever it was that woke him. Were his instincts playing tricks on him?

He didn't want to believe that, because like any lawman he relied heavily on his hunches to tell him how to proceed in his investigations. If he were to start conjuring up threats where none existed . . .

He sat up suddenly in bed, his hand reaching out in the darkness to close around the butt of the Colt. He had coiled

43

his gun belt and placed it on the chair beside the bed within easy reach. He slid the revolver from the holster with a whisper of metal against leather.

Nothing happened. The room was as silent and empty as ever.

Longarm muttered a curse. He had been sleeping without the sheet over him, wearing only the bottom half of a pair of long underwear. He was starting to swing his legs out of bed to stand up when he heard something rasp on the floor right under his feet.

He jerked backward, kicking his legs in the air instead of lowering his feet to the floor. So violent was his reaction that he turned a somersault and almost went off the other side of the bed. He flailed with his free hand, caught hold of the wooden headboard, and stopped himself from falling. He pulled himself back onto the center of the bed.

Sweat beaded his face, but not because the night air was hot and sticky and close in the hotel room.

His coat was hung on the back of the chair. He reached over to it and found a small tin box of matches in one of the inner pockets. He took a lucifer from the box and snapped his thumbnail against the head to light it. As the sulphur match flared into flame, Longarm leaned over and let the light from it shine on the floor beside the bed.

A colorful but ugly snake lay there, about two feet long, its slender body ringed by bands of red, yellow, and black scales.

"Red and black, you're safe, Jack," recited Longarm under his breath. "Red and yellow, kill a fellow."

The red and yellow bands on the body of the snake on the floor touched each other. It was an eastern coral snake, one of the most venomous serpents in the whole country. Longarm had seen men die within minutes from the bite of one of these little bastards.

The snake's head was black and blunt and rather small, not like the thick, wedge-shaped head of a rattler. That

44

didn't make it any less deadly, though. Longarm searched his memory, trying to recall everything he could about coral snakes.

A rattlesnake could strike the length of its body and was aggressive about doing so. A coral snake couldn't do that, and that was probably the only thing that had saved Longarm's life. He had come damned close to putting his feet down on the thing. A rattler would have struck at him as soon as he came within reach of it. The coral snake probably wouldn't bite him unless he stepped on it.

So he was safe as long as he stayed on the bed. When the match went out he struck another one and used it to light the lamp on the bedside table. In the glow that rose from the lamp he saw another red, yellow, and black snake on the floor on that side of the bed.

How many of the blasted varmints were in here, and what was he going to do about them?

He didn't ask himself how they had gotten into the room. A narrow balcony ran along the front of the hotel, just outside his window. Someone had crept along there, probably carrying the snakes in a tow sack, and had dumped them through the open window.

He thought about shooting the two that he could see, then getting up carefully to check for more snakes. But if he missed, or even if he didn't, the bullets would probably penetrate the floor and then the ceiling of the room below him. There was no telling who or what else they might hit. He couldn't take that chance.

If he'd had a bowie knife or something like that he could have tried to cut off their heads. The only knife he had, though, was a folding one with a short blade. Not much good for lopping off snake heads.

That left him with only one option. He reversed the gun in his hand and gripped it by the cylinder and barrel. After making sure the hammer was sitting on an empty chamber, he carefully leaned over and picked up one of his boots with his other hand. Then he perched on his knees on the edge of the bed, knowing that if he lost his balance and toppled off, the fall might prove fatal.

Longarm didn't like snakes. He had a healthy respect for them, and he knew that some of them even served useful purposes. But some atavistic and instinctual part of him just pure-dee hated the scaly bastards.

So with a surge of anger that had surely come down through the ages from his barbarian ancestors, he slammed his boot heel on the snake's body a few inches behind the head, pinning it to the floor, and then bashed the hell out of it with the butt of his gun.

He drew his arm back to strike again but saw that a second blow wouldn't be necessary. The first one had crushed and flattened the snake's skull. The rest of its body whipped around wildly as the muscles fought a futile battle against the knowledge that it was dead, but after about a minute the writhing stopped.

Satisfied that he had disposed of one threat, Longarm moved over to the other side of the bed. The snake he had seen earlier was still there. Action had settled his nerves a little, so without hesitating he pinned that one down and walloped the life out of it, too. Now he had a dead coral snake on each side of the bed.

He was wondering if there were any more in the room when he saw a black head and a few inches of striped body poke out from under the bed and then retreat out of sight again.

"Shit!"

The exclamation was a heartfelt one.

Longarm used a corner of the sheet to wipe sweat off his face. If he had slept through the night and then gotten out of bed in the morning, there was a good chance he would have stepped on one or more of the snakes. It was an uncertain way of killing a man, but if it worked there would be nothing to prove it wasn't an accident. No evidence would point to murder. After all, it wasn't unusual for a snake to get in some place where it wasn't supposed to be.

"Damn you, Duquesne," muttered Longarm. Maybe he wasn't being fair; maybe he was misjudging the sheriff. But he was convinced in his own mind that Duquesne was responsible for these unwelcome nocturnal visitors.

Or maybe it had been the limping man, who was still an enigma.

Longarm sat there for a few minutes and pondered the situation. His feeling of alarm grew as he thought about it. Whoever wanted him dead had seen him with Natalie. The killer might want to dispose of her, too.

And there was an endless supply of coral snakes in the swamp.

No snakes were on the floor between the bed and the door, but at least one was underneath the bed. If he got up, would it come after him? He doubted it, but he was no expert on such things. In the past he had seen copperheads chase a person. Maybe coral snakes were that aggressive, too.

He would have to risk it. He had to get to Natalie and make sure she was all right.

Longarm drew his legs up and rose to his feet. Standing on the bed, he moved to the foot of it. One good leap would carry him almost to the door. The snake on the bed wouldn't have a chance to get close enough to bite him.

He took a deep breath and jumped.

When he was in midair he saw the third coral snake crawling out from under the foot of the bed. As soon as his bare foot hit the floor he was reaching for the doorknob.

It refused to turn. The door was locked, he remembered with a groan.

And the key was in his coat pocket, across the room on the chair.

Longarm spun. The snake was only a couple of feet from him, writhing toward him. Without thinking about what he was doing, he bent over and grabbed at it with his free hand, snatching it up from the floor. He had caught hold of it close enough behind the head that it couldn't turn and bite his hand. That didn't stop it from wrapping its body around his forearm. A feeling of revulsion went through him. His hand tightened.

The snake's writhing and whipping became more frenzied. Longarm felt delicate bones cracking and snapping under his grip. The snake's mouth opened and closed, but there was nothing for it to sink its venom-laden fangs into.

Longarm kept an eye on the floor in case any more snakes emerged from hiding, but this one seemed to be the last. He maintained his death grip on it until the snake's muscles finally relaxed and it slipped off his arm to hang limp and motionless from his outstretched hand. He didn't drop it until he was sure it was dead.

Then, being careful to avoid stepping on any of the carcasses, he hurried to the chair, retrieved the key from his coat pocket, and unlocked the door.

He had banged around and caused enough of a commotion killing the snakes that he thought someone else in the hotel might come to investigate, but the corridor was deserted when he stepped out into it. The hour was late, so everyone else was sound asleep, he supposed.

He closed his door behind him and catfooted along the hall to Natalie's room. As he paused in front of her door he tried to remember the layout of her room. The window was to the left, opening onto the alley that ran beside the hotel. No balcony out there, but a fella could put a ladder against the wall and climb it. Wouldn't be easy to do while carrying a sackful of snakes, but it could be done.

And it was doubtful that Natalie's senses would be sharp enough to wake her at the first sign of trouble, as Longarm's had. That meant she was probably still slumbering peacefully in there. If he banged a fist on the door and called her name, that would startle her and she would jump out of bed. . . .

Longarm gave a little shake of his head. Couldn't risk that. Instead he rapped softly on the door and called in a voice little louder than a whisper, "Natalie! Natalie, wake up!"

No response, so he knocked again, and this time as he pressed his ear against the door he heard a drowsy murmuring from inside. He put an imperative edge in his voice but kept it calm and steady so she wouldn't panic as he said, "Natalie, you've got to wake up, but don't get out of bed!"

"Custis?" Her voice was thick with sleep. "Custis, is that you?"

"Wake up, Natalie," he told her. "You've got to listen to me."

"For God's sake, Custis, go back to your room! You can't come in at this hour."

"Natalie, listen to me, please. Can you light your lamp without getting out of bed?"

"What?" She sounded confused, and rightfully so.

"Light your lamp, but whatever you do, don't get up. Keep your feet in the bed."

"Custis, you've lost your mind—"

"Just do as I say."

He held his breath as he listened for the scratch of a lucifer being lit. He heard it a few seconds later, along with the clink of the lamp's chimney being replaced. Then Natalie exclaimed, "Oh, my God, what—"

A terrified shriek ripped from her throat, followed by four words that turned Longarm's blood to ice in his veins.

"It's in the bed!"

So much for being slow and quiet and careful. He grabbed the knob with his left hand, twisted as hard as he could, and slammed his left shoulder against the door with all the power in his rangy frame behind it.

49

The door gave with a splintering of wood and then slammed open. Longarm stumbled into the room and by the flickering light of the lamp saw Natalie huddled against the headboard, her legs drawn up as far as they could go. On the foot of the bed lay a coral snake, its head no more than eighteen inches from Natalie's bare left foot.

"Don't move!" shouted Longarm. He had no choice but to risk a shot. The gun in his hand roared.

The snake's stubby black head exploded as the bullet struck it. The scaly body flipped into the air.

"Custis, look out!" Natalie screamed.

Longarm looked down at the floor and saw another of the venomous serpents closing in on his foot. With an involuntary yell he leaped high in the air. When he came down his feet were spread about as wide as his long legs would allow. He bent and struck with the barrel of the Colt, bringing the gun muzzle down with such force behind the snake's head that the head was severed from the body.

That made two, but he didn't know how many more were in the room. Stepping wide around the still biting head, he searched the floor and looked under the bed. He didn't see any more snakes.

Rapid footsteps sounded in the hall. The desk clerk from downstairs appeared in the doorway, no longer looking sleepy. The middle-of-the-night gunshot had chased away his drowsiness. In his excitement, he yelped, "What's going on here?"

Longarm put up a hand to stop him from charging into the room. "Better hold on there, old son," he said. "You might step on something you don't want to."

The clerk looked down at the floor and gulped. The body of the decapitated snake still writhed, and the creature's mouth still opened and closed, although that motion was now growing weaker. "What the hell!" the clerk said.

"I wouldn't advertise this, if I was you," said Longarm.

"Snakes in every room won't get you much business, I reckon."

From the bed, Natalie said, "Custis . . . ?"

He turned to look at her. She wore a long, high-necked nightgown and had tugged it down so that it covered all of her except her feet. Her thick ash-blond hair was loose around her shoulders now, and even under these circumstances Longarm took note of how appealing her tousled appearance was. It was a rare woman who could be startled out of a sound sleep and look attractive, but Natalie Stoneham managed to do so.

"Is . . . is it dead?" she went on.

Longarm nodded. He went over to the bed and used the barrel of his gun to lift the limp body from the bloodstained sheet. The sheet and the mattress underneath it had bulletholes in them now, as well, but that had been unavoidable.

"Don't worry," he told her. "He can't hurt you now."

"But . . . but I don't understand! How did snakes get in here? We're on the second floor."

Longarm looked at the window. He had lowered the shade earlier, but it was raised more than halfway now, as was the window. The window in his room had been open only a few inches, just wide enough for whoever was on the balcony to get the mouth of the sack through it and dump the deadly contents.

In here, the killer had risked raising the window and the shade, figuring that Natalie was less likely to wake up. Somehow, he had managed to toss one of the snakes all the way onto the bed.

There was no telling how long Natalie had shared the bed with her scaly visitor. It was pure luck that she hadn't shifted around in her sleep, kicked at the snake, and caused it to bite her. If that had happened, she would have been dead by now.

At that thought, a rage that was both hot as hades and

51

cold as ice began to form inside Longarm. Somebody would pay for what had nearly happened tonight.

From the doorway, the clerk asked in a weak voice, "Would . . . would you like to move to another room, ma'am?"

Natalie closed her eyes and sighed. "Yes, please," she said.

Chapter 6

Sheriff Remy Duquesne came into the hotel dining room the next morning while Longarm and Natalie were eating breakfast. Both of them had moved to other rooms after the incident the night before. Longarm didn't know about Natalie, but his sleep had been restless and dream haunted. He sure didn't like snakes.

But a big platter of eggs, flapjacks, and steak, washed down with several cups of hot black coffee, had gone a long way toward restoring his vitality. When Duquesne approached the table, Longarm looked up and gave him a curt nod.

"Sheriff."

"Good morning, Marshal," Duquesne said. "I trust you slept well."

Longarm's eyes narrowed. "Not too well. Seems that Miss Stoneham and I both had some unwelcome visitors. The kind with scales and fangs."

"Yeah, I heard something about that," said Duquesne as he pulled out one of the empty chairs and sat down without being invited. "I'll look into the matter."

"I reckon you should, since it was attempted murder and all."

"Oh, now, I'm not sure you can just make an accusation like that." Duquesne signaled to the waitress to bring him a cup of coffee. "There are a lot of snakes around these parts. People get bit from time to time. Doesn't make it murder."

Longarm agreed there were plenty of snakes around here—and one of them wore a badge. But he didn't say that. Nor did he mention the scratches he had found in the white-wash on the outside wall of the hotel just under the window of Natalie's room. Someone had placed a ladder there, just as he had thought. He didn't trust Duquesne enough to share any of the details of his investigation with him.

Matter of fact, he didn't trust Duquesne at all.

The sheriff took a sip of the coffee the waitress brought him and then said, "You haven't had much luck since you came to Saint Angelique, Marshal. First old Jacquard is killed before you even get a chance to ask him about the fella you're looking for, and then you almost get yourself bit by a coral snake. Maybe you should give some thought to going back where you came from."

"Without finishing my job?" Longarm shook his head. "I don't think so."

"But you won't ever find that fella. He's long gone. The swamp got him. He's never coming back." Duquesne shrugged his thick, sloping shoulders. "It's a shame, but that's just the way it is."

Longarm glanced at Natalie and hoped she could hold her emotions in check. She was pale but controlled. She looked down at what was left of her food and pointedly paid no attention to Duquesne.

"Well, I gave you the best advice I know how to," the sheriff said. "Whether or not you take it is up to you." He gulped down the rest of his coffee and got to his feet. "Maybe I'll go see if I can find some coral snakes to question."

When Duquesne had lumbered out of the dining room, Natalie said quietly, "I don't like that man."

"Neither do I," said Longarm.

"I think I agree with you. He had something to do with Matthew's disappearance. At the very least, he knows more than he told you. Otherwise he wouldn't be trying to get you to leave town."

Longarm smiled. "Now you're thinking like a lawman."

"What are you going to do now?"

"Keep poking until I've got the hornets stirred up enough to come out of their nest." Longarm drank the last of his coffee. "Then I reckon I'll start swatting."

Although during breakfast he had tried to bring up the subject of Natalie returning to New Orleans and leaving the search to him, she had deftly sidestepped it. Longarm set that aside for the time being and walked down the street to the livery stable to check on his horse. He thought that Natalie ought to be safe enough in the hotel in broad daylight.

The old black hostler was still working at the stable. He gave Longarm a grin and said, "I been takin' good care o' that bay o' yours, mister."

"I never doubted it," Longarm told him. He looked in the stall where the horse was munching on some oats and nodded in satisfaction. Then he turned to the hostler and went on, "You've been around here for quite a spell, haven't you, old-timer?"

"I reckon you could say that," the hostler replied with a chuckle. "I was born up at Coffin Hill, on Bayou Noir, in the year o' our Lord eighteen fifteen."

"What's Coffin Hill?" asked Longarm.

"The ol' Blanchard plantation. I was one o' the lucky ones, got to stay there with most o' my family 'stead o' bein' sold off and tooken God knows where. When the war come along and us slaves got freed, I come down here an' went to work for Mr. Lon Williams, the fella who owns this here stable. Been workin' for him ever since."

"I've heard that after the war some of the freed slaves stayed on the plantations where they'd been all their lives."

"Some of 'em, maybe." The old man's voice hardened. "Not the ones who lived at Coffin Hill. They left soon's the Yankee troops come in and said they could."

Longarm didn't want to stir up bad memories for the old-timer, so he changed the subject by saying, "Since you've been around Terrenoire Parish for so long, you must've heard all the stories about Jean Lafitte's treasure being hidden somewhere in these parts."

"That ol' pirate? Shoot, yeah, I done heard the stories. Don't know as I believe 'em, though. Seems to me that if there was pirate loot cached 'round Bayou Noir, somebody would've found it 'fore now. Been more'n sixty years since Lafitte was around here."

"That's the second time you've mentioned Bayou Noir," said Longarm. "What's that?"

"Black Bayou. Bubbles up somewhere deep in the swamp and f vs down from the northeast to run into the Atchafalaya. Mostly swamp around it, but they's some plantation land, too. Them ol' stories 'bout Jean Lafitte say he hid his treasure somewhere close by Bayou Noir, but I ain't never seen no treasure."

Since the experiences of the night before had proven to Longarm that he could still trust his hunches, he played another one and said, "I asked you yesterday whether or not you'd rented a horse to a young fella who wanted to go into the swamp. You said you hadn't."

"An' that's the truth, mister, swear to God."

"But I didn't ask you if you'd *talked* to a fella like that."

The old-timer pursed his lips and didn't answer. Longarm knew how closemouthed a lot of former slaves could be. The harsh lives they had led on the plantations had taught them not to volunteer information.

But finally the old man nodded and said, "I talked to him."

"He asked you about Jean Lafitte's treasure, didn't he?"

"Are you after that pirate loot, mister?"

"I don't care about it one way or the other. It's the young man I'm looking for. Did you tell him about the old stories and send him up Bayou Noir?"

"I didn't send nobody nowhere," the old-timer answered emphatically. "If that boy went up Bayou Noir, he done it on his own."

Longarm felt his pulse quickening. This was the first real lead to Matthew Chadwick he had found in Saint Angelique. With deliberate abruptness, he changed tacks by saying, "I guess you heard that Pierre Jacquard got himself killed last night."

The old man caught his breath. "I heard."

"Did you know Jacquard?"

"I knowed him. An' while I'm sorry to see any man pass on, I ain't a-gonna mourn that ol' Frenchman too much. Never liked him. He was no better'n he had to be, an' he was so fond o' money that he'd do most anything for it."

"Like go into the swamp with that young fella we were just talking about and lead him into a trap?"

The hostler shook his head. "I don't know, mister. I honestly don't. Could've happened that way. Jacquard knew his way around these parts, and I heard that the young fella was lookin' to hire hisself a guide. But I minds my own business much as I can, so I just don't know what happened."

Longarm decided that the old man was telling the truth. He didn't think there was any more information to get from him on this subject.

But there was still another matter.

"I asked you yesterday about a man with a limp—"

"And I done told you then, I don't know nobody like that," the old-timer broke in. "Still don't."

The stubbornness in the hostler's voice was so apparent that Longarm knew he'd be wasting his time trying to force an answer. The old man had dug in his heels.

"You mentioned a plantation called Coffin Hill. Is it still there?"

"It's there, all right. Still in the Blanchard family. Mr. Tristam Blanchard runs it now. Was his daddy who was the master when I was a boy there." The old-timer shook his head. "He was a bad man. Lots o' bad men back in them times." He turned away. "Still lots o' bad men now."

"Is there a road to Coffin Hill?" Longarm asked him.

Without turning around, the old man nodded. "They a road, sort of. More of a trail. You can get a wagon over it, long as it ain't too big."

"Does it follow that Bayou Noir you mentioned?"

"Most o' the way." The hostler looked back over his shoulder. "You ain't thinkin' o' goin' up there, are you, mister?"

"I've got to find that young fella, or at least find out what happened to him."

The old-timer's voice shook a little. "Strangers go up Bayou Noir, sometimes they don't come back. *Lots* o' times they don't come back."

"I've got a job to do," said Longarm.

"They's all kinds o' trouble up there, trouble you don't know nothin' about."

"Like that limping man?"

The old man swung around. "Don't you be talkin' 'bout him! Bad things happen to folks who see the limpin' man!"

Longarm smiled faintly. "I thought you said you didn't know him."

The old-timer snatched up a pitchfork and stalked toward a pile of hay in the back of the barn. "I ain't talkin' to you no more. Anything you do, it'll be on your head, mister. Not mine."

"Fine," said Longarm. "Saddle my horse when you get a chance. I'll be riding out directly."

The old man just snorted and plunged the pitchfork into the hay.

Longarm left the livery stable and walked back to the hotel. Along the way, he mulled over what he had learned this morning.

It seemed likely that Matthew Chadwick had gone up Bayou Noir in search of Jean Lafitte's treasure, and Pierre Jacquard had gone with him. Jacquard had known what happened to Chadwick. That gave someone— Duquesne?—a motive to kill Jacquard.

But he didn't need to get too far ahead of himself, thought Longarm. It was possible that Jacquard's murder had nothing to do with Chadwick's disappearance. Someone could have had an entirely different motive for cutting the old man's throat.

The timing of the murder was suspicious, though. Jacquard had been killed the same evening that Longarm arrived in Saint Angelique. Until he found out something that pointed in a different direction, the theory Longarm had come up with sounded reasonable to him.

The next step was to take a ride up the Bayou Noir trail himself.

Before he did that, he wanted to be sure that Natalie Stoneham was safe. He found her sitting in the lobby of the hotel, looking at a three-week-old Baton Rouge newspaper.

She lowered the paper and leaned forward in her chair. "Have you found out anything else?" she asked.

"I may have a lead on which direction your cousin went when he left here," said Longarm. "I intend to check it out. First, though . . . how did you get here?"

She frowned at him. "What do you mean?"

"You said you arrived in Saint Angelique yesterday. How?"

"I took the train from New Orleans to Grosse Tete and rented a buggy there."

That was the little town where Longarm had left the train and rented the bay. Obviously, Natalie had come through there a little ahead of him.

"You drove a buggy down here? By yourself?"

Natalie smiled. "I know, you don't think a woman should be doing such things. It's not safe, and it's certainly not proper for a female to travel alone."

"Especially one who ain't even carrying a gun."

"That reminds me . . ." She took his watch, chain, and derringer out of her bag and held them out to him. "I need to return these things to you."

He took them and snugged watch and derringer back in their accustomed places in his vest pockets. "I'll ride to Grosse Tete with you," he said, "then come back down here and get on with the investigation."

"What? I'm not going back to Grosse Tete. I'm going with you, Custis."

He shook his head. "Not hardly. It ain't safe, and I don't need to be saddled with no female."

Her eyes flashed with anger, but she kept it under control. She said, "I told you, Matthew is like a brother to me. I have to help him, and if it's too late for that, at least I have to know what happened to him."

"I'll see that you're informed of whatever I find out—"

"And what guarantee is there that *you'll* come back from the swamp, Marshal?"

"I thought you were calling me Custis."

"And I thought we were becoming friends."

He scrubbed a hand over his face in frustration. "I'll take you to Grosse Tete—"

She held up a hand to stop him. "And you know perfectly well that as soon as you're out of sight I'll come after you."

"Not if I put you on the train and make sure you leave."

"You'll have to hogtie me to do that," she challenged him. "And I'm not sure my uncle Tobias would be happy to hear that his niece had been manhandled that way."

Unfortunately, she was right. While there was a chance

Senator Chadwick would be pleased that Longarm had kept his niece out of danger, you never could predict exactly how a politician would react. The senator could just as easily get a burr under his saddle about it.

"Damn it, the swamp's no place for you."

"Think about it this way, Custis . . . Would you rather have me where you can keep an eye on me, or would you prefer that I was off on my own, perhaps getting into trouble where you wouldn't be able to help me out?"

It seemed to Longarm that he'd had this same identical argument with any number of headstrong gals in the past. For some reason he drew pretty, troublemaking females like a lodestone drew iron filings.

"All right," he said. "Is your buggy down at the livery stable?"

"That's right."

"We'll have it hitched up when I get my horse. But there are a couple of things you've got to agree to before you can come along."

"Anything you say, Custis . . . within reason."

He looked at the nice traveling outfit she wore. "How do you feel about wearing pants?"

Her eyes widened. "Like a man's trousers, you mean?"

"That's right. If you need to move around in a hurry, long skirts and petticoats just get in the way."

"Well . . . it's rather scandalous. But I suppose I could wear trousers if you think it's best."

Longarm nodded. "I noticed a general store across the street. Reckon they'll have guns for sale. I want to buy you a pistol and maybe a rifle."

She agreed to that with less hesitation than she had about the pants. "All right. That's probably a good idea. There are a lot of dangerous things in the swamp, I expect."

"More'n you know," grunted Longarm.

It took about an hour to get Natalie properly outfitted. In

61

the general store, Longarm bought her a pair of whipcord trousers, a couple of linsey-woolsey shirts, a wide-brimmed brown felt hat, and a pair of high-topped boots. For weapons he picked out a Colt New Line revolver in .32 caliber, small enough for her to handle but powerful enough to put a man down, especially if he was hit in the right place, and a short-barreled Winchester carbine in .44-40, so that it would fire the same rounds that his rifle took. As they walked down to the livery stable, Longarm had her carry the carbine so that she could start getting used to the weight of it.

The old hostler's eyes widened in amazement as he saw Natalie. He drew Longarm aside and said in a low, urgent voice "Tell me you ain't a-gonna take that lady into the swamp, mister. Please tell me you ain't."

"I don't want to, old son, but she ain't giving me any choice," explained Longarm. "She's stubborn as a mule, and if I don't take her, she's liable to just follow along behind me and get into even worse trouble."

The old-timer shook his head. "Lord, Lord. You best watch after her mighty close. And watch your own back, too."

"I'm sort of in the habit of doing that," Longarm assured him. "Now, we'll need my horse and the lady's buggy."

The old-timer gripped Longarm's arm. "One more thing. You get in trouble up yonder on Bayou Noir, you look for a fella called Bullroar. He'll help you, if'n he can. Tell him Josiah says so."

"That's you? Josiah?"

The old man nodded. "Yeah. Him an' me are old friends."

"Thanks. I'll remember that."

"I sure wish you'd change your mind 'bout this, mister."

"Maybe I should, but I've got a job to do."

"No job's worth meetin' up with what you might run

into in that swamp." A shiver ran through the old man as he said it.

Longarm turned his head and looked at Natalie Stoneham. As she smiled at him, he hoped he wasn't making the worst mistake of his life—and hers.

Chapter 7

Reluctantly, the old man told them how to find the trail that led to Bayou Noir and the Coffin Hill plantation. It branched off the main road north of Saint Angelique. As Longarm and Natalie reached the trail later that morning, the big lawman glanced around. In this land of moss-laden trees and marshes, truly distinctive landmarks were few and far between, but he thought this was just about the place where he had heard the bobcat's cry and seen the limping man the previous evening.

Longarm wished he knew who that son of a bitch was.

Natalie's rented buggy was pulled by a single horse. As Longarm reined in and studied the trail, he didn't think that the vehicle would have any trouble negotiating it, although there might be places where it was so narrow he would have to ride ahead of the buggy, rather than beside it.

"You sure you want to do this?" he asked Natalie.

She looked at the path. The trees grew together above it, creating a canopy that threw thick shadows on the trail. It reminded Longarm of a dark tunnel with something unknown, but probably not good, on the other end. After a moment Natalie gave a nervous nod.

"This is our best chance of finding Matthew, isn't it?"

"I think so," said Longarm.

"Then I have to do it." Natalie steeled herself with a visible effort and flapped the reins against the back of the buggy horse. "Let's go."

They moved onto the trail, and within fifty yards it seemed like they were in a different world, one where the bright sunshine had been replaced by shifting shadows and a green glow caused by light filtering through the ceiling of branches and leaves and vines and creepers. Insects buzzed through the air and small animals rustled in the thick undergrowth. There was no wind. A sultry stillness hung over the landscape.

A snake of some sort slithered across the trail in front of them and disappeared into the brush. Natalie said, "Ugh."

"That wasn't a coral snake or a cottonmouth," said Longarm, "so it was probably harmless."

"I don't care. After last night it would be all right with me if I never saw another snake again."

Longarm felt pretty much the same way. He knew they would likely see more snakes before they got out of the swamp.

After about half a mile they came to a stream. The trail turned to follow it. Longarm brought his horse to a halt and sat there for a moment looking at Bayou Noir.

He could see how the stream got its name. The water was so dark it appeared black as it flowed sluggishly between twisting banks lined with moss-covered trees. The bayou was about forty feet wide. Longarm couldn't tell how deep it was, but most of these lowland streams were fairly shallow. Probably no vessels would be able to navigate it except the flat-bottomed craft called pirogues, used by Louisianans to ply the bayous that meandered through the swamps.

"That's one of the ugliest rivers I've ever seen," commented Natalie.

"You won't get any argument from me," said Longarm as he watched what looked like a small log drift along the surface of the black water. He knew it wasn't a log at all. It was a crocodile or an alligator, swimming lazily with most of its body under the surface as it looked for prey.

Longarm didn't point out the creature to Natalie. She had enough to make her nervous without worrying about crocs and gators. He turned to the northeast and said, "Come on. That plantation ought to be this way."

"Do you think the people there will know anything about Matthew?" asked Natalie as she got the buggy horse moving again.

"Only one way to find out."

They rode along in silence for a while, until Natalie finally said, "You know, it's sort of odd that you and I both arrived in Saint Angelique to search for Matthew on the same day."

"I had the same thought," Longarm agreed, "but when you consider he's been missing for about a month, it's not that strange. Takes a while for word to get back to civilization from a place like this, where things haven't changed much for a hundred years or more. There's no telegraph or railroad line into Saint Angelique. How'd you find out about your cousin being missing, anyway?"

"Matthew was supposed to be back for my aunt's birthday party two weeks ago. When he didn't show up, Uncle Tobias and Aunt Margaret knew something was wrong. Uncle Tobias sent a man to look for him, but the man couldn't track him any farther than Saint Angelique. He got back to New Orleans about ten days ago."

Longarm nodded. "Reckon your uncle started burning up the wires between there and Washington, trying to find somebody else to take up the search."

"And that would be you."

He laughed. "That would be me. What about you?"

"When I heard about it, I wanted to come look for

Matthew right away. But I told myself that I couldn't do such a thing. I'm a mere woman, after all." Sarcasm dripped from her words. "Being a Southern belle can be very frustrating, Custis. There are all sorts of things you're not supposed to do."

"I wouldn't know about that."

"Trust me. Anyway, it took me a few days to work up the nerve to make the trip over here on my own. I finally did, though. And then fate brought us together in Saint Angelique."

Longarm wasn't sure he believed in fate, but he knew coincidences happened. His line of work made him naturally suspicious of such things, but in this case he thought Natalie was telling the truth. He was going to accept her story, anyway, until she gave him reason not to.

They had brought some supplies with them from the general store, and although the lack of direct sunlight under the trees made it difficult to tell what time it was, Longarm called a halt when he thought it was around the middle of the day. A check of his watch told him that he was correct.

"We'll stop and eat some lunch," he said. "I don't know exactly how far it is to that plantation, but I hope we can get there before nightfall."

"I do, too." Natalie lowered her eyes. "If not, we'll have to spend the night out here on the trail."

They ate the bread and salt pork they had brought along, and Longarm used his knife to open a couple of cans of peaches. Back in his cowboy days, canned peaches had been the greatest treat that a puncher on a long trail drive could have, and they were good here, too. Natalie ate hers and then followed Longarm's example and drank the juice from the can. When she was finished she wiped the back of her hand across her mouth.

Longarm grinned at her. "You're getting the hang of it,"

he told her. "Being a lady is fine, but there's times when it's best not to worry about such things."

"I have a feeling that traveling with you is going to be quite an education, Custis."

There was more than one way a fella could take a comment like that, he thought.

Then suddenly he forgot all about it as Natalie dropped her empty can, pointed, and cried out, "Custis! Look over there!"

Longarm whirled around and looked where she was pointing. He saw the shadowy figure dart into the cover of the trees. It was moving fast, but not so fast that he didn't recognize the limping gait.

"It's him!" exclaimed Natalie. "The man I saw at Mr. Jacquard's shack last night!"

And the fella Longarm had seen on the road, too. He ran after the man, pulling his Colt from the crossdraw rig as he approached the trees.

The limping figure was completely out of sight by the time Longarm plunged into the trees. Fingers of moss brushed at his face. It was even darker once he was off the trail. The air was thick with the dank smell of rotting vegetation.

He stopped and listened, thinking that surely the man he was chasing wouldn't be able to travel through this jungle without making any noise. But as Longarm stood there he didn't hear a thing. Even the birds and the small animals were quiet now.

He catfooted forward, trying to be quiet so he wouldn't give away his own position. The soggy ground squished under his boots. As he placed each foot carefully, he wondered if there was any quicksand in these parts. He didn't like quicksand any more than he liked snakes.

He came to a clearing but didn't step out into it immediately. Instead he stood there for a moment at the edge of the trees, still in shadow, and let his eyes search for any sign of the limping man. He was about to decide that the hombre had gotten away when he saw a sudden flash of movement on the far side of the clearing.

The man stepped out of the trees and looked around. Longarm couldn't see his face because the battered, broad-brimmed old hat that the man wore shaded it. The brim dipped down in front far enough to conceal some of his features, too.

In addition to the hat, he wore a long coat that hid his clothing. The coat had to be stifling in this hot, sticky weather. Longarm had taken off his coat, rolled it up, and put it away in his bag as soon as he and Natalie left Saint Angelique that morning.

As he stepped out of the trees, Longarm leveled his gun at the mysterious figure and said, "Hey! Hold it right there, mister!"

The limping man whirled. Whatever was wrong with one of his legs didn't slow him down any as he darted back into the shelter of the trees. Longarm had been tempted to squeeze off a shot, but just before his finger tightened on the trigger he had decided that he couldn't risk it.

He wanted the limping man alive to answer questions, so he couldn't take a chance on accidentally killing him.

Lowering the Colt, Longarm started across the clearing at a run. He had taken only a couple of steps when his feet suddenly sunk. Water splashed up around them. The clearing was actually a marsh, but Longarm hadn't been able to see the water because of the thick grass. The mud on the bottom sucked hard at his boots, trapping them. He lost his balance and had to windmill his arms to keep from falling forward onto his face.

When he was able to stand up straight again, he worked his feet free from the clutching mud and slogged on across the clearing at a much slower pace. The limping man would be long gone by now, he thought bitterly.

And yet when he stepped onto more solid ground, he heard brush crackling up ahead of him, not too far away. Maybe the limping man had waited to see if Longarm was going to get stuck in the mud.

Or maybe he was doubling back to try an ambush.

When Longarm reached the trees on the far side of the marsh, he paused to listen. The crackling in the brush had stopped. He pressed his back against the mossy trunk of a tree and thought about Natalie.

What if the limping man had shown himself only to draw Longarm away from her? He might have circled around and be back there at the trail now, doing God knew what to the young woman. Longarm was faced with a choice—go forward and continue trying to find the limping man, or turn back and rejoin Natalie to make sure she was safe.

More sounds came from the brush, and they were still ahead of Longarm. That made up his mind for him. He slipped forward, the gun held ready in his hand.

Seeing more than ten or twelve feet in here was impossible. Longarm had to track his quarry by sound. The limping man wasn't running now, but rather moving more slowly, maybe trying to keep quiet about it. But it couldn't be done. Longarm heard quiet splashing and the rustle of brush being pushed aside.

Of course, the limping man probably heard *him*, too.

The noises stopped and so did Longarm. He waited with the patience of a man who knew from experience that being still and quiet was sometimes the only thing that saved a fella's life.

He didn't hear a thing. Silence reigned now.

Had the limping man gotten away? Longarm didn't see how that was possible. He glided forward. He knew he was taking a chance, knew that he might be walking into a trap, but he had come too far to turn back now. If there were answers up ahead, he was determined to get them.

He stepped out of the trees and stopped short before he splashed into a stream even smaller and murkier than Bayou Noir. It was barely ten feet across. Longarm looked down at the bank and saw marks in the mud. Something had been pulled up there. A boat or a raft, maybe. The limping man could have had a pirogue stashed here, and he had poled silently away down the creek in it.

"Damn it," muttered Longarm. He walked up and down the stream for several minutes, searching for tracks, but he didn't find any. Nor were there any footprints on the far bank, which he could see easily from where he was.

Like it or not, the limping man had given him the slip.

He holstered the Colt and turned to go back the way he'd come. A frown creased his forehead as he realized that he didn't know exactly where that was. All the flowers and trees and thickly hanging strands of moss looked alike. When his gaze dropped to the ground he saw that only the most recent tracks he had made were still visible. The others had already filled in with mud and water. This ground was too soggy to hold prints for very long.

He couldn't tell for sure where he had come out of the trees. And that meant he didn't exactly know how to get back to the place where he had left Natalie.

This was crazy, he told himself bleakly. He was a frontiersman, with a frontiersman's sense of direction. He couldn't have gotten lost that easily.

Yet this land of swamps and marshes was much different from the prairies, deserts, and mountains to which he was accustomed. The terrain itself conspired to confuse a man. So much of it looked alike, and there were no high places where he could climb to orient himself. The trees kept him from seeing the sun, so he couldn't even steer by that.

Longarm pulled a bandanna from his pocket, took off his hat, and mopped sweat from his face. Insects buzzed around his ears, and mosquitoes that he crushed when he wiped his face left bloody streaks on the cloth.

Scowling in frustration, he tucked the bandanna away and said, "The hell with it." He walked back into the trees at a place that looked vaguely familiar.

He had gone only a hundred yards or so when he figured out that he had made a mistake. None of this looked familiar to him; on the other hand, it all looked *too* familiar. But he was convinced this wasn't the way he had come, so he stopped and turned around.

That was when he realized that he didn't even know how to get back to the little stream where he had lost the limping man.

Longarm stood there thinking for a moment. Standing still was the worst thing he could do, he decided. If he kept moving, chances were that sooner or later he would come across some place he recognized. That was all it would take to tell him where he was, and then he could get back to Natalie.

By now she had to be wondering what had happened to him, and he regretted the fact that she was probably worried. He hoped she had enough sense not to come looking for him. Then they would both be lost in this leafy labyrinth.

He stiffened as several loud noises suddenly rang out. The reports were somewhat muffled by the heavy, damp air, but they were definitely gunshots. They sounded like they came from a Winchester, and he immediately thought of the carbine he had bought for Natalie earlier in the day.

A different gun roared. Longarm broke into a run, trying to follow the sound of the shots. The guns fell silent, though, so after a moment he wasn't sure if he was still going in the right direction or not.

He kept moving, knowing that he couldn't stop. He struggled through the brush. The vines and the creepers almost seemed to be alive and striving to hold him back. He wished he had a machete to hack his way through them. If he had stopped to think about it back in Saint Angelique, he probably would have bought one, just in case he ran into a situation like this.

Finally—and somewhat to his surprise—he burst out of the undergrowth and stumbled onto the trail where he had left Natalie. Breathing heavily and sweating from his exertions, Longarm looked around for her. He spotted the buggy about a hundred yards to his right, but he didn't see Natalie anywhere around it.

Somebody must have grabbed her, he thought wildly. The damned limping man? That was the most likely answer. Longarm broke into a run toward the buggy, calling, "Natalie! Natalie!" as he ran.

He was almost there when he heard her scream. She ran out of the trees on the far side of the trail from Bayou Noir. A man lunged after her, reaching for her. Longarm brought up his Colt, intending to ventilate the son of a bitch before he could recapture Natalie.

She screamed, "Custis! Look out!"

Too late, he tried to turn as he realized the real threat was behind him. That was when a huge weight crashed into him, driving him forward and bearing him to the ground.

74

Chapter 8

The breath was knocked out of Longarm when he hit the trail, but his brain still worked clearly enough for him to realize that someone was lying on top of him, trying to pin him down. He drove an elbow up and back and felt the point of it sink into a man's belly. The man who had tackled him grunted in pain.

Longarm got his hands and knees under him and heaved himself upward. With a startled yell, the man on top of him fell off and rolled to the side. Longarm went the other direction and scrambled to his feet. He knew he had dropped his gun when he was knocked down, and he looked around for it now, hoping he could find it before somebody opened fire on him. There were at least two enemies here, the one who had tackled him and the one who had chased Natalie out of the trees.

That man had caught her, Longarm saw now. She was struggling to break free.

He spotted his Colt lying on the ground and started for it, but before he could reach the gun more men stepped out of the concealment of the trees. Longarm heard the metallic sound of guns being cocked, and a voice saying, "Hold it, mister! We ain't lookin' to shoot you, but we will if we have to."

Longarm froze. The odds had just increased to five to one, and three of those men, the ones who had just emerged from the trees, were covering him. Two had shotguns and the other one held a rifle. At this range, they could blow him to shreds without any trouble.

The man he had elbowed in the gut was still on the ground, but he was struggling to catch his breath and get up. "Lemme have him, Davey," he said. "I wanna pound on him for a while."

"Ain't no need for that," said the man who had spoken to Longarm. "He ain't puttin' up a fight no more."

"I don't care. He hurt me."

The man called Davey smiled. "You'll get over it." He turned his head and called, "Oscar, get over here. Bring the girl."

The fifth man tightened his grip on Natalie and forced her to walk with him as he joined the others. Longarm looked her over carefully and asked, "Are you all right?"

She was pale but appeared to be unharmed. Her hat had been knocked off and her hair tumbled loose around her shoulders.

"I'm fine," she said, "just mad at being handled so roughly."

"Sorry, ma'am," said Davey. "You was the one who started shootin' at us. We couldn't take any chances on you blowin' holes in us."

Longarm looked over their captors. None of them appeared to be the man he had pursued earlier, but he couldn't be sure of that since he had never gotten a good look at the limping man's face. As far as he could tell, none of these gents walked with a limp. They wore ragged trousers and shirts, and their shoes and boots had holes in them. All five of them were dark-skinned, the hues ranging from the blue-black of pure African lineage to the lighter brown of mulattoes and quadroons. They were all between twenty and thirty years old, which meant they had probably been born as slaves before the war.

Davey picked up the gun Longarm had dropped and tucked it behind his belt. "You folks just settle down and we'll talk a mite," he said. "Ain't lookin' for no trouble."

"Do you plan to rob us?" asked Natalie. "We don't have much money—"

"We ain't thieves," Davey broke in. "We look like thieves to you, ma'am? Must have, 'cause you started shootin' at us soon's you saw us."

Longarm was starting to get the idea that this might be just one big misunderstanding. As worried as Natalie had undoubtedly been when he went off in pursuit of the limping man and didn't come back, it was possible she had opened fire on these men without provocation.

"Listen, we're not looking for trouble, either," he said. "Why don't you unload my gun and give it back to me, and we'll go on our way and you can go yours."

Davey seemed to be considering it for a moment, but then he shook his head and said, "No, I reckon we best get some things straight first, and one of 'em is what are you folks doin' out here?"

"We're looking for my cousin," Natalie answered before Longarm could say anything. "Have you seen him? His name is Matthew Chadwick."

Longarm frowned. He might have been tempted to come up with some answer that would have concealed their real purpose, but it was too late for that now. Natalie had blurted out the truth.

"Never heard of him," Davey said. "What's he look like?"

Quickly, Natalie described her cousin. The five men shook their heads.

Davey continued as their spokesman. "Sorry, I don't reckon we ever run into him. But from the sound of it, he didn't have no business out in the swamp, neither."

"Are you saying we have no right to be here?" asked Natalie.

"Sayin' it ain't smart for folks who don't know their way around these parts to wander around gettin' into trouble. I reckon we best take you back to Pont-a-Mousson and let Bullroar figure out what to do with you."

That comment caught Longarm's interest. He had no idea where or what this Pont-a-Mousson place was, but the old-timer at the livery stable in Saint Angelique had said that someone called Bullroar might be able to help them if they got into trouble.

"We don't want to go with you—" Natalie began stubbornly.

Longarm silenced her with a hand on her arm. "Don't mind the lady," he said to Davey, getting an angry glare from Natalie for his trouble. "We'll be glad to go with you."

"But Custis—" she began.

"No need in everybody getting all worked up," he said as he looked at her, trying to get her to understand that she needed to play along with him. "I'm sure we can get everything straightened out in no time."

"Oh, all right," she muttered. "But I want my rifle back."

"That be up to Bullroar," said Davey.

With the five men surrounding them, Longarm and Natalie walked back to the buggy and Longarm's horse. He helped her into the vehicle and then untied the bay's reins from the bush where he had tethered them when he and Natalie first stopped for lunch. He didn't mount up, though. Davey and the other men were on foot, so Longarm fell in step with them as they started walking northeast along the trail.

This was the direction he and Natalie had been going anyway, he told himself. They hadn't lost anything except a little time.

As they walked along the trail, Davey said, "Why were

you runnin' around out in the woods, mister? You lucky you didn't step in no gator hole."

"I was trying to catch up with somebody," said Longarm.

"You mean they's somebody else out here that ain't got no business bein' here?"

Longarm took a chance. "Yeah. A man in an old hat and a long coat. A man with a bad limp."

All five men stopped in their tracks, forcing Natalie to haul back on the buggy horse's reins to keep the animal from running into them.

The man who had scuffled with Longarm said in a voice hushed with awe, "You was chasin' the limpin' man?"

"You know him?"

"We don't know who he is," said Davey, "but we know enough to know we wouldn't want to catch him. Bad things happen to folks when they mess with the limpin' man."

Old Josiah back in Saint Angelique had said almost exactly the same thing.

Oscar, the man who had recaptured Natalie when she tried to get away from him, said, "Folks who see the limpin' man disappear, and they never come back."

A couple of the others nodded solemnly.

"We don't know that the limpin' man got anything to do with that," Davey said. "Sure is mighty suspicious, though. He comes sneakin' 'round Pont-a-Mousson at night, like some sort o' haint, and the next mornin' somebody be gone."

"What is this Pont-a-Mousson?" asked Longarm.

"Place where we live. Come on. We be there before too much longer."

Davey started walking again. The others followed.

After a few minutes, Longarm ventured another question. "Do you know a man named Pierre Jacquard?"

One of the men spat into the bayou, as if just hearing Jacquard's name put a bad taste in his mouth.

"Jacquard lives in Saint Angelique," said Davey. "We

know him. He ain't no account. Does some huntin' and trappin' muskrats. But he'll steal anything that ain't tied down, too, and you don't want him comin' 'round your womenfolks, 'cause he ain't to be trusted."

Longarm said, "You don't have to worry about that anymore. He's dead."

The men didn't stop walking this time, but they all looked at Longarm. "Dead?" asked Davey. "What happened to him?"

"Somebody cut his throat last night."

One of the men snorted and said, "Had it comin', he did."

"And the limping man was seen near his shack about the time it happened, too," added Longarm.

That brought several mutters from the men. Longarm thought some of them might have been prayers, as if they were trying to ward off evil.

Bayou Noir twisted and turned so much that it seemed like they were walking miles just to cover what would be a short distance in a straight line, thought Longarm. Finally, though, the group went around a bend in the trail and came in sight of a cluster of shacks and shanties constructed of scrap wood, tar paper, and irregular pieces of tin. Most of them sat up on stilts, because this lowland had a tendency to flood during every heavy rain.

"This here's Pont-a-Mousson," announced Davey.

Longarm thought it was a pretty fancy name for a place that was far from fancy.

"Come on," Davey continued. "We take you to see Bull-roar now."

The young man walked toward a building Longarm hadn't seen at first, because it was partially concealed behind the shacks and backed up to the bayou. It was an old frame house with a sagging porch that ran along the front. Not as big as a plantation house, it had two stories and was

80

still a good-sized structure that had been nice in its day, before years of neglect and disrepair had set in.

"Hey, Bullroar," Davey called as the group came up to the porch.

A moment later the front door opened and a tall, lean white man stepped out of the house. He was around fifty, Longarm judged, with a wild shock of graying sandy-colored hair that had receded somewhat from his forehead. He wore an old white suit over an open-throated white shirt. Lifting a hand in greeting as he looked curiously at Longarm and Natalie, the man said, "Hello, Davey. I see we have visitors."

Bullroar wasn't exactly what Longarm had expected. His voice held a faint French accent, and he had the dreamy-eyed look of a man who possessed some culture and education.

"We run into 'em on the Bayou Noir trail," explained Davey. "They're lookin' for somebody."

"My cousin," Natalie spoke up. "His name is Matthew Chadwick. Have you seen him?"

Bullroar still smiled pleasantly but didn't answer the question. "Please, won't you come in, *mes amis*?"

Longarm knew that meant "my friends." He was reserving judgment on just how friendly this fella really was, though.

Longarm helped Natalie down from the buggy. Davey took Longarm's gun from behind his belt and handed it to Bullroar. One of the other men had Natalie's pistol and rifle. He turned them over to the Frenchman, too.

"We had to take their guns away," said Davey. "Didn't want nobody gettin' trigger-happy."

"Caution is always a good thing." Bullroar smiled at Longarm and Natalie. "Don't worry, your weapons will be returned. *If* I am satisfied that you mean no harm to me and my friends."

81

"We're not looking for trouble," Longarm told him.

Bullroar held out a hand as he opened the door. "Come in. Tell me all about why you have come to Pont-a-Mousson."

Longarm felt the planks of the porch give a little under his weight as he crossed them. In damp country like this, it was hard to keep the rot out of wood. The house seemed to still be in good enough shape not to be in any danger of collapsing, though.

The atmosphere inside was one of shabby gentility. The furnishings had been expensive when they were new, but time and humidity had taken a toll on them. Bullroar ushered Longarm and Natalie onto an old divan and sat down opposite them in a wing chair with a lace cover over its back.

"Introductions seem to be in order," said the Frenchman. "I am Andres Boulware."

"So that's where the name 'Bullroar' comes from," said Longarm. "I got to admit, it didn't seem to fit you too well."

Boulware smiled. "Yes, my friends have corrupted it somewhat, but I take no offense from that. Their feelings toward me are affectionate. I gave them a place to live when they had nothing, and for that they are grateful. Together, we have formed a community here." The long, slender fingers of one hand drummed on an arm of the chair. "But you have not told me your names."

"I'm Custis Long, and the lady is Miss Natalie Stoneham." Longarm didn't mention that he was a deputy U.S. marshal.

"And you say you are searching for Miss Stoneham's cousin?"

"That's right," said Natalie. "He was last seen in this area about a month ago."

Boulware spread his hands. "A month is a long time, especially in the swamps. I am sorry, Miss Stoneham, but if your cousin has been missing for that long, it is very likely some misfortune has befallen him."

"I know," Natalie said with a determined nod. "People keep telling us that. But I want to find out what happened to him anyway."

"Why did he come here?"

Natalie opened her mouth to answer, but before she could speak, Longarm held out a hand to stop her. He said, "Before we get into that, I'm a mite curious about this place and how it came to be here."

Boulware smiled. "And therefore you want to hear more before you decide whether or not to trust us."

Longarm shrugged. "I'm in the habit of eating an apple one bite at a time."

"A colorful expression. I believe I get your meaning, M'sieu Long. And I have no objection to indulging your curiosity. I am a Creole. My family has been here in Louisiana for more than a hundred and fifty years, dating back to the time when France first controlled this territory. Once the Boulwares owned a great deal of land on both sides of Bayou Noir and had a fine plantation."

Boulware steepled his hands in front of his face as he leaned back in the chair.

"Over the years, though, my ancestors lost control of more and more of their land through financial reversals, until finally all that was left was this small section along the bayou. I left for a time as a young man and was educated in New Orleans. When I came back I brought a bride with me . . . but she succumbed to a fever a few years later, leaving me alone here."

"How sad," murmured Natalie.

"It was," agreed Boulware, "and for a time I admit that I indulged too freely in wine and self-pity. Then the war came, and the Yankee soldiers." He looked at Longarm. "Did you take part in that conflict, M'sieu Long?"

83

"Yeah, but don't ask me which side I fought on," replied Longarm. "It was a long time ago, and I sort of disremember."

Boulware chuckled. "I maintained a certain neutrality, myself. The plantation days were over for the Boulware family long before the war ended them for everyone else in the South. We had had no slaves for years, so there was nothing for me to lose. In the days following the war, however, many freed slaves began to travel down the bayou. They were lost souls in a way, with no idea where to go or what to do. So I decided to offer them . . . a home."

"You founded this little village, in other words."

Boulware smiled and nodded. "And I named it Pont-a-Mousson in honor of the village in France where my ancestors came from before they traveled to the new world." He sat forward now with his hands clasped between his knees. "The war displaced many people, *mes amis*, not just freed slaves. Pont-a-Mousson became a haven for anyone who no longer had any place to call home. We farm, we fish, we live a simple but rewarding life here. Our people are Creoles, Cajuns, and former slaves, and we have learned to live with each other in peace."

"Sounds fine," said Longarm, "but human nature being what it is, I'd bet a hat that trouble started cropping up sooner or later, didn't it? That's why you folks are a mite edgy these days."

Boulware gave a solemn nod and said, "Some of our young people have disappeared in recent years. Never very many, and not too often, but enough of them and often enough so that everyone is frightened. 'Edgy,' as you put it."

"Scared of the limping man," said Longarm.

Boulware caught his breath and frowned. "What do you know of him?"

"Not a blasted thing other than the fact that we've caught sight of him a few times. He seems to be able to disappear whenever he wants to. I reckon he knows his way around these parts really well."

"I fear that he comes from Coffin Hill."

It was Longarm's turn to frown. "You mean the Blanchard plantation?"

Boulware slammed a fist against his knee and said, "I mean the home of the devil himself!"

Chapter 9

The vehemence of the Frenchman's reaction surprised both Longarm and Natalie. Longarm said, "I reckon you don't get along too well with that fella Blanchard."

"Neither Tristam Blanchard nor his overseer Hank Hennigan are deserving of the name human being, in my opinion," Boulware said stiffly. "Most of the freed slaves who came to settle at Pont-a-Mousson were from Coffin Hill. Do you know how that plantation got its name, M'sieu Long?"

Longarm shook his head.

"Some say it is because the small knoll where the big house is located is shaped something like a coffin . . . but the former slaves claim it is because so many of their number were beaten or starved to death or died of some other disease brought on by neglect and abuse. Coffin Hill is a terrible place, *mes amis*. You must avoid it if you can."

Longarm wasn't sure that was going to be possible. He still had to find Matthew Chadwick, and so far the trail—nebulous though it might be—led toward the Blanchard plantation.

"We'll bear that in mind," he said noncommittally. "Fella who works at the livery stable down in Saint Angelique didn't have anything good to say about Coffin Hill, either."

With a visible effort, Boulware forced himself to relax and smiled. "You mean Josiah? A fine old gentleman. He would have been welcome to stay here with us, but he wanted to move on. We have remained in contact, though."

Longarm nodded and said, "Fact of the matter is, he told me that if Miss Stoneham and I got in trouble up here, we ought to look you up. He thinks you're trustworthy . . . and I reckon he's probably right."

"Your reserve is understandable." With a shrewd look in his eyes, Boulware added, "But I will admit that I am quite curious as to why Miss Stoneham's cousin came to Bayou Noir in the first place."

Longarm looked at Natalie, who said, "I think we should tell him, Custis. He seems like an honorable man."

Longarm agreed and said to Boulware, "Miss Stoneham's cousin Matthew Chadwick, who has been calling himself Matthew Charleston, was looking for Jean Lafitte's treasure when he disappeared."

"Treasure?" Boulware laughed. "The only treasure up here is the simple life that we lead in Pont-a-Mousson among friends and family."

"You haven't heard that Lafitte is supposed to have cached part of his loot up here?"

Boulware waved a hand. "Of course I have heard the old stories. But they are baseless."

"How do you know that?"

"Well . . . I don't, of course. But I don't believe the old tales. Surely if the treasure existed, it would have been found by now."

Others had made that same argument. For all Longarm knew, they were absolutely right. But evidently Matthew Chadwick had believed in the stories, and that was really all that mattered.

"Maybe so," he said, "but we're more interested in finding Matthew Chadwick than we are in any treasure. We'd be much obliged for any help you can give us."

"Of course. I shall spread the word among my people and find out if any of them saw this fellow you're looking for. Can you describe him to me?"

Natalie told Boulware what her cousin looked like. The Frenchman nodded as he committed the details to memory.

Longarm leaned forward and said, "If you'll give us our guns, I reckon we'll be going on our way. . . ."

"To Coffin Hill?" Boulware asked sharply.

"That's right."

Boulware shook his head. "I am afraid that is impossible."

Longarm felt anger welling up inside him. The Frenchman put up a polite front, but if he figured on keeping them prisoner here, he was going to have a fight on his hands.

But Boulware went on, "It is too far for you to reach today. If you must go there—and I still advise against it— you would be wise to spend the night here and then continue your journey in the morning. That way you will arrive at Coffin Hill during daylight hours." He shook his head. "You would not want to try to follow the trail in darkness. Danger lurks once the sun is down in these parts."

He probably had a point there, thought Longarm. And Natalie had been worried about having to spend the night on the trail, he recalled. He exchanged a glance with her and saw her head move in a tiny nod. She wanted to stay.

Longarm didn't fully trust Boulware yet, although the Frenchman's story rang true to him. But given the circumstances, remaining overnight at Pont-a-Mousson might be the smartest thing to do.

"We'll still want those guns back," he said, his tone firm enough that it left no room for argument.

"Certainly. And this will give me a chance to question my people as well and see if I can find out anything about your poor missing cousin, Miss Stoneham."

"We appreciate that," Natalie said.

Boulware smiled and casually waved a hand. "It is nothing. And of course, you will be my guests for dinner this evening."

He returned their guns to them, and Longarm felt better once the Colt was back in its holster where it was supposed to be. He never felt quite right without the weight of the gun on his hip.

"Our humble village does not offer much in the way of amenities," Boulware went on, "but please feel free to look around and visit with the people. You will find them quite friendly once I have assured them that you represent no threat to them and their families."

Longarm asked him, "Did it occur to you that Matthew Chadwick's disappearance might be tied in somehow with the folks who have vanished from here?"

Boulware's face took on a grim cast as he nodded. "Indeed it has, *mon ami*. Perhaps if you find out what happened to M'sieu Chadwick, you will discover the answers that my people need as well."

The afternoon passed in surprisingly pleasant fashion. Longarm and Natalie walked around the little community of Pont-a-Mousson and found themselves greeted by everyone in a friendly fashion. Clearly, Boulware had kept his word and let everyone know that the two visitors were welcome.

Although their circumstances were modest, most of the people who lived here wore smiles on their faces. Children ran and played in the village, and laughter was heard frequently.

The people grew solemn, though, when Longarm brought up the subject of the ones who had disappeared over the past couple of years. He kept a rough count in his head and realized that nearly two dozen individuals had vanished. Most were young men between fifteen and twenty-five years old, but a few young women had disappeared, too. Some of their family members cried when they talked about it, but others were angry.

And all of them were scared. Longarm sensed that. No one knew when it would happen again, or who would be the next person to disappear.

As he talked to the citizens of Pont-a-Mousson, his conviction grew that these incidents were tied in with the mystery surrounding Matthew Chadwick's fate. He believed in coincidence, but there was too much of it in this case. The easy answer would be to say that the limping man had gotten all of them.

The people were afraid of the limping man, that was for sure. Only a few of them would admit that they had seen the mysterious figure sneaking around the village in the past. It was as if they thought they would be the next to vanish if they acknowledged him.

Late that afternoon, they were summoned back to Andres Boulware's house by the young man called Davey. Boulware sat in the parlor where they had talked earlier, and standing next to his chair was a young mulatto boy.

"Thomas here seems to be the only one who saw your cousin when he passed through this area, Miss Stoneham," explained Boulware. "Please tell our new friends what you told me, Thomas."

The boy looked shyly at the floor as he said, "I was huntin' for crawdads down on the bayou when these two fellas come ridin' by. I knowed one of 'em. . . . He was that Mr. Jacquard fella from down to Saint Angelique. I didn't like him. I was scared o' him."

Thomas looked at Boulware for encouragement, and the Frenchman nodded and said, "Go on."

"But the gent with him was a whole heap nicer. He stopped an' talked to me for a while, real friendly-like. He wanted to come here to Pont-a-Mousson an' visit with folks. But that Mr. Jacquard, he wouldn't let him. Said they had to be movin' on if they was gonna get where they was goin' afore it got dark. So they rode on, and I seen 'em headin' down the go-'round."

"What's the go-'round?" asked Longarm.

Davey said, "It's a trail some folks take to Coffin Hill, if'n they don't want to take the trail that follows the bayou. Cuts some distance off, the way the bayou winds back and forth."

Longarm nodded in understanding. "That's how they got past Pont-a-Mousson without anybody seeing them."

"Undoubtedly," agreed Boulware. "Go on, Thomas. What did this second man look like?"

"Well, he was a white man, with dark hair and them bushy whiskers on the sides o' his face. A really handsome gent, seemed to me like."

"That was Matthew," Natalie said. She looked at Longarm with excitement gleaming in her eyes. "Now we know he was up here, and that he was headed to Coffin Hill."

"I reckon we do," he said. "And we've got a witness, for the first time, who puts Jacquard with him."

Boulware said, "Davey tells me you said that M'sieu Jacquard is dead?"

Longarm nodded. "Someone murdered him last night. Probably somebody who had something to do with Matthew Chadwick's disappearance." He kept to himself the suspicion that Sheriff Duquesne was involved.

Boulware smiled at the boy and asked, "Can you tell us anything else, Thomas?"

"No, sir. That be all I know."

"Very well, then. Thank you for being honest with us." The youngster left the room. When he was gone, Boulware looked at Longarm and Natalie and went on, "Sad though I am to say it, it looks more than ever as if your quest has only one logical destination."

"Coffin Hill," said Longarm. "And from what you said earlier, it might as well be hell."

"Or worse," said Boulware. "Hell on earth."

• • •

They ate dinner with Boulware, and not surprisingly the fare included rice, beans, and crawfish from the bayou. Longarm was more of a steak and potatoes man, but the food was good.

After the meal, Boulware said, "I've had my maid prepare rooms for both of you upstairs. I hope that's satisfactory."

"Yes, of course," said Natalie. "Thank you for your hospitality, Monsieur Boulware."

The Frenchman smiled. "You might as well call me Bullroar like everyone else, my dear."

"Oh, I couldn't do that. The name doesn't suit you at all."

"Whatever you please. Now, if you'd care to join me, I have some excellent cognac stored away. I brought it with me when I returned here from New Orleans. You're the first visitors I've had in a long time who might truly appreciate it."

Longarm was more of a Maryland rye drinker, but he had to admit that the cognac Boulware poured for them was mighty smooth and good. The label on the fancy bottle read Martel, whatever that meant.

Natalie enjoyed the liquor, too, maybe a mite too much. She laughed a little more than usual, and when the evening was over and she started upstairs to her room, Longarm thought there was more of a sway in her walk. He remained downstairs to smoke a cheroot with Boulware.

As the two of them sat in the parlor, Boulware said, "I hope you will forgive me, M'sieu Long, but I feel that you have not told me the complete truth. Were you hired by Miss Stoneham to accompany her on her search for her cousin? Or is this more of an official assignment for you?"

"Why would I be assigned to look for Chadwick?"

"Because you are either a military man or an officer of the law," stated Boulware. "I can see it in your bearing and in your eyes."

Longarm shrugged. "I'm a deputy United States marshal."

"Why is Matthew Chadwick so important that—" Boulware stopped short, then went on, "*Mon dieu!* He is related to Senator Chadwick!"

"The senator's son," confirmed Longarm. "That's why I have to either find him or figure out what happened to him. It was just luck that I ran into Miss Stoneham and she had the same idea."

"Good luck . . . or bad?"

"I don't reckon I know for sure about that yet."

Boulware sat there silently for a moment, then said, "Marshal, something evil is going on up at Coffin Hill. While you are there, will you see if you can find out anything about the ones who have vanished so tragically from Pont-a-Mousson?"

"It was already in my mind to do that," Longarm said.

"*Merci*. I fear that if this plague is not stopped, it will continue to take my people."

"You don't have any idea what's happening to them?"

Boulware shook his head. "Only that it is bad. It might be best if Miss Stoneham were to remain here. . . ."

Longarm grunted and said, "Good luck talking her into that."

"Yes, I know. She strikes me as a very determined young woman. Be careful, both of you . . . or you, too, may vanish."

Longarm took that as a genuine warning, not a threat. He was convinced that Boulware wasn't mixed up in whatever was going on around here. The Frenchman was too obviously pained by the tragic, mysterious disappearances.

A short time later, Longarm went upstairs to turn in for the night. Earlier, the maid had shown them which rooms were theirs. When he went to his now, he wondered if there was a lock on the door. He trusted Boulware and the people of Pont-a-Mousson, but out of habit he liked to make sure he didn't get any unwelcome visitors during the night.

Especially after those coral snakes had come calling the night before.

If the door didn't have a lock, surely there would be a chair he could wedge under the knob, he thought. And he planned to have his Colt close by if he needed it, maybe even under his pillow.

But as he turned the knob and opened the door, he saw that he already had a visitor. The lamp on the bedside table was lit, and its warm glow spilled over the bed like Natalie Stoneham's ash-blond hair spilled over the pillow at its head. The sheet was pulled up over her, but it was low enough to reveal smooth, rounded arms and sleek, bare shoulders.

She smiled up at him and said, "I was afraid you were going to stay downstairs talking to M'sieu Boulware all night, Custis."

Longarm's eyes narrowed. Those bare shoulders of Natalie's were mighty pretty, and so was she with her hair loose like that. But he had never been the sort of man who would take advantage of a woman, so he said, "You had too much of that cognac to drink, Natalie. You're drunk, and you don't know what you're doing."

"I most certainly do know what I'm doing," she shot back at him, "and I'm not drunk. I had just enough cognac to convince me that I should stop suppressing my impulses and do what I've been wanting to do ever since I met you."

She threw the sheet aside, revealing that she was gloriously nude in Longarm's bed.

"Make love to me, Custis. Now."

Chapter 10

She was as beautiful as Longarm had figured she would be if he ever saw her with her clothes off. Her body was very fair-skinned without being unhealthily pale. Her breasts were the size of apples, and as she cupped them and squeezed them herself, he saw that they were about as firm as apples, too. Pale pink nipples crowned each globe of female flesh.

From there his gaze wandered on down, over her taut, flat belly to the triangle of fine-spun hair where her thighs came together. It was a shade darker than the hair on her head. Her thighs opened and closed, giving him glimpses of the moist lips of her sex. She moved her right hand from her breast and used it to reach between her legs and stroke herself. She began to breathe harder.

Longarm's jaw tightened, as did the trousers over his groin. Natalie was making it damned difficult for him to be a gentleman about this.

He said, "What was all that talk about being proper and avoiding any scandal? You acted sometimes like you were afraid I was about to jump on you and ravish you if I got half a chance."

"You've got that . . . all wrong, Custis," she panted in

her growing excitement. "I was afraid if I didn't . . . keep everything under control . . . that *I* would ravish *you*!"

He had to admit that she didn't sound all that drunk, just randy as hell. She might not have shed her inhibitions if she hadn't had a couple of snifters of cognac, but the liquor wasn't making her do anything she didn't really want to do.

Her hand was moving faster between her legs now, and her bottom bounced up and down on the bed. She closed her eyes. Her breath hissed between tightly clenched teeth.

"Hell with it," muttered Longarm. He reached for his string tie and jerked it loose, then started unfastening the buttons of his shirt.

Out of deference to the thin walls, Natalie clamped her lips shut as she brought herself to her first culmination. As her back arched, cords stood out on her neck from the strain of the ecstasy that flooded through her.

Longarm continued peeling off his duds as he watched her, and by the time he was naked his shaft was fully erect and jutted out from his groin like a long, thick bar of iron. As he eased onto the bed, Natalie opened her eyes. They widened even farther when she saw his stiff manhood.

"My God, Custis," she murmured. "I assumed you would be well built, but I didn't dream that you'd be so . . . so . . . I don't know if I can get all of that monster inside me!" She reached out to clutch eagerly at him. "I'm certainly willing to try, though!"

He moved closer to her as she encircled his shaft as best she could with both hands. Her fingers didn't quite meet. She stroked it up and down, her touch sending waves of pleasure cascading through him.

He slipped a hand between her thighs. She closed them on it, trapping his hand with the soft warmth of her legs. After a moment her thighs parted, and he slid his fingers over her sleek skin until he encountered the wet heat at her core. She was already drenched with the juices her earlier climax had brought forth. He slipped two fingers into her, causing her to gasp as he began to explore her femininity.

While his fingers stroked in and out, his thumb found the sensitive nubbin of flesh at the top of her opening and strummed it. Her fingers tightened on his shaft. After a moment she sat up and said, "Keep playing with me, Custis," as she leaned over to lap her tongue around the head of his cock.

His fingers moved faster as she continued to lick him. Her pelvis thrust against his hand. She moaned softly, opened her mouth, and closed her lips around his shaft. She began to suck urgently on it, and then she spasmed around his fingers as another climax washed over her.

Longarm pulled back before he erupted in her mouth. Natalie sagged back on the bed as if all her muscles had gone limp. Her legs were splayed wide open. Longarm moved over her, poised in position for a second as he brought the head of his shaft to her opening, and then sheathed himself inside her with one smooth thrust. She was so wet that he went into her with ease.

Natalie's eyes flew open again. She might have cried out or moaned, but before any sound could come from her lips Longarm's mouth found hers in an urgent, heated kiss. Her lips parted eagerly and their tongues found each other, darting and swirling in a sensuous dance. First he explored the warm, wet cavern of her mouth, and then she returned the favor.

And all the while he pumped his manhood in and out of her core, filling her with each thrust and then pulling back so that he could plunge deep within her again. Natalie's hips came up off the bed as she met Longarm's thrusts and gave as good as she got.

They fell into the timeless, universal rhythm as if they had been coupling for years, rather than this being the first time. Her arms wrapped tightly around his neck, and her knees rose and her ankles locked together over his surging buttocks. When their mouths finally parted, she panted, "Custis, oh, Custis!" in a whisper.

Longarm felt his climax boiling up as he pounded into her. Just before it was ready to burst, he drove as deep as he could for a final time and held himself there. Natalie climaxed underneath him as his seed exploded from him in a series of throbbing, white-hot blasts. Their juices mixed together in a torrent that flooded her to overflowing.

Both of them shuddered as their culmination rippled through them. Longarm was careful to keep his knees and elbows on the bed so that he wouldn't crush her with his weight. He brushed kisses across her lips, her nose, her cheeks, her eyes. She gave a long, drawn-out sigh of satisfaction as she lay there with her eyes closed.

After a moment Natalie opened her eyes and whispered, "You just wear a girl out, Custis. But it's the best tired I think I've ever felt." Then her eyes widened with realization. "Good Lord, you're still hard! You . . . you can't possibly be ready to go again this soon!"

Longarm chuckled. "Give me a few minutes. I ain't as young as I used to be."

She laughed and pushed his shoulder. "Get off me, you magnificent brute," she said.

Longarm moved so that his still semi-erect shaft slipped out of her wetness. Despite the fact that she was the one who had told him to get off, she made a little sound of disappointment when he slipped out. He rolled onto the bed beside her and propped himself on an elbow so that he could use his other hand to fondle her. Both of them were sweating from their exertions in this sultry climate.

Longarm cupped each of her breasts in turn and stroked the pink nipples with his thumb. He caressed the line of her jaw and slipped his hand behind her head to hold it as he gave her a long, intense kiss. She explored his body at the same time, her movements languid as she ran her hands over his powerfully muscled frame and reached between his legs to cup the heavy sacs that hung below his cock.

"You're getting harder," she observed.

"I reckon you have that effect on a fella."

"I think you *are* going to be ready again in a few minutes. I wouldn't have believed it. Now I'm sorry I didn't ravish you last night. Think of all that time we wasted."

"I don't reckon either of us were exactly in the mood," said Longarm dryly, "after those snakes paid us a visit."

Natalie frowned. "You *would* have to remind me of that. That was an awful experience."

"And from the way ol' Bullroar was talking, it's liable to get even worse up at Coffin Hill."

Natalie sat up abruptly and said, "I don't care. I know I'm not a lawman like you, Custis, but I have instincts, too, and they're all telling me that we'll find out what happened to Matthew when we get to Coffin Hill."

Longarm sat up, too, and drew her into his arms. As she rested her head on his shoulder, he stroked her hair and said, "I hope you're right about that. I surely do."

They made love again a short time later and then dozed off in each other's arms. An unknowable time after that, Longarm woke up with his erect shaft in Natalie's mouth again. He was lying on his back, so he grasped her hips and urged her around so that her thighs were straddling his face. As she sucked him enthusiastically, he used his thumbs to spread open her sex so that he could lick it from one end to the other and spear his tongue into her. She moaned around his manhood and sucked even harder.

Not surprisingly, they climaxed into each other's mouth a short time after that.

Longarm was about to doze off again when he heard something that made his head jerk up off the pillow. Natalie noticed his reaction and asked groggily, "Custis, wha . . . what's wrong?"

"Somebody's hollering out there," he replied, his voice taut. "Some sort of hell's busted loose."

Longarm sat up and swung his legs off the bed. As he did so, he remembered what he had almost stepped on the night before. He had left matches on the chair beside the bed, along with his gun. He snatched one of them up and snapped it into life.

The floor next to the bed was empty of everything except his boots.

Relieved, he bolted to his feet and started pulling on his clothes. He could hear the shouting a little more clearly now, and he thought somebody was saying, "The limping man! The limping man!"

Once he had his shirt and trousers on and had stomped his feet down into his boots, he grabbed the Colt without taking the time to buckle on the gun belt. "Stay here," he told Natalie as he headed for the door.

"Custis, be careful," she called after him.

"I plan to," he said over his shoulder. "You better get dressed, too, and keep your gun handy, just in case."

He went out and hurried down the stairs. A lamp still burned in the parlor, and he saw a book lying open on the table beside the chair where Boulware had been sitting earlier. The Frenchman must have been reading when the commotion started outside.

Longarm stepped onto the sagging porch. He saw a lantern's bobbing yellow light as someone carrying it hurried between the cabins. A group of people seemed to be forming in the center of the community. More lanterns converged on the spot.

Longarm went down the porch steps and walked quickly toward the gathering. "Who's that?" yelled somebody, and a rifle suddenly blasted.

Longarm crouched instinctively for a second, but he straightened as he realized that the fire from the weapon's muzzle had been pointed upward. Someone had knocked the rifle barrel toward the sky just before the trigger was pulled.

That someone was probably Boulware, because a second later the Frenchman said angrily, "*Mon dieu*, hold your fire! That is our visitor, M'sieu Long. He is not the limping man!"

"Damn right," said Longarm as he stalked up to the group. "I don't really blame folks for being a mite trigger-happy, though, with everything that's been going on around here. I reckon somebody spotted the limping man sneaking around the village?"

Boulware still wore a white shirt and the trousers of his white suit. The pale clothing caused him to stand out in the darkness. He would make a good target if the limping man or somebody else lurking in the shadows decided to take a potshot at him.

"Davey saw him," answered Boulware, and that brought frightened mutters from the others gathered around.

"That's right," said the young man. "I heard somethin' skitterin' around outside my cabin, thought it might be a possum or a muskrat. So I stepped out to shoo it away, and that was when I seen him. He ran off, but he was sure limpin'. Figured I'd better spread the warnin'."

"Oh, Lord!" one of the women cried. "He's come to take us all away."

"That limpin' man, he be ol' Satan's right bower, I guarantee," added another man, his accent telling Longarm that he was one of the community's Cajun settlers.

"He's a man just like any other man, and if'n I can get him in my sights, I'll prove it," vowed Davey. He hefted the shotgun that he held in his hands.

Boulware was armed, too, with an old, long-barreled pistol. Longarm motioned to him and Davey and said, "Let's take a look around. These other folks better go on back to their homes, though. Don't want anybody making any mistakes and shooting somebody they shouldn't."

The Frenchman nodded. "Do as M'sieu Long suggests, everyone. If the limping man is still here, we will find him, have no worries about that."

As the crowd broke up, still scared and muttering among themselves, Longarm, Boulware, and Davey began their search of the village. Boulware had a lantern in one hand, the old pistol in the other. He walked in the center with Longarm on his right and Davey on his left.

The three men searched from one end of Pont-a-Mousson to the other and found no sign of the limping man except some footprints around Davey's shack. As Longarm studied them in the light from Boulware's lantern, he saw that the print of the left foot was deeper than that of the right.

He pointed that out and said, "The varmint puts a lot more weight in his left foot than he does his right. That matches up with what I've seen of him. It's his right leg that's hobbled."

"He was after me," said Davey in a hushed voice. "His tracks are only here around my cabin, and he ran away into the woods when I discovered him." The young man's voice rose. "He come to get me. He was gonna carry me away like he done with all the others!"

Boulware tucked his pistol behind his belt and then gripped Davey's arm. "Steady, my young friend," he said. "We don't know why he was here, but he is gone now." The Frenchman's tone grew more grim as he went on, "We must make sure everyone in Pont-a-Mousson is accounted for."

Longarm knew what he meant. They had to check on the other citizens of the village to be certain the limping man hadn't done his dirty work on anybody else before Davey discovered him skulking around the settlement.

That took another half hour and was up to Boulware and Davey, since Longarm didn't know everybody who lived here. He accompanied the two of them, though, just in case they ran into any trouble.

When they were finished with the chore, Boulware sighed in relief. "Everyone is where they should be," he said, "including the children. The limping man stole no one from Pont-a-Mousson tonight."

"Wish I'd got a good shot at him," said Davey. "I'd've put a load of buckshot in his other leg, so's it'd match the bad 'un."

Boulware chuckled. "My young savage. Go back to your cabin and sleep well for what is left of the night, Davey. I do not think the limping man will trouble us again tonight."

"You can't know that," Davey said skeptically.

"No, but I can hope."

Davey shrugged and nodded. Longarm and Boulware stood there watching until the young man reached his shack safely and went inside.

As they turned back toward Boulware's house, the Frenchman said, "I am sorry your slumber was disturbed as well, M'sieu Long. I trust your room is sufficiently comfortable."

"Mighty comfortable," he said, without adding that Natalie had found it to be so as well.

"What about Miss Stoneham?"

The question made Longarm frown, since it was almost like Boulware had just read his mind. But the expression on the man's face as they went into the house was blandly innocent.

"I'm sure her room is fine."

"No, no, I mean, did you see her before you came outside? Was she frightened by the shouting?"

"Oh. Yeah, I looked in on her," said Longarm, stretching the truth a mite now. "I told her I'd see what was going on and that she ought to stay put. She seemed to be all right. She doesn't spook easy."

"She must be a very brave young woman, to venture up Bayou Noir in search of her cousin like that."

"She's determined, no doubt about that," agreed Longarm.

Boulware blew out the lantern. "Well, I shall return to my book," he said as he gestured at the chair in the parlor. "I am afflicted with difficulties in sleeping. It has been so ever since my poor wife passed away."

"Sorry," muttered Longarm. He left the Frenchman and went upstairs, anxious to make sure for himself that Natalie was all right. She was the only one in the village they hadn't checked on, he realized.

When he opened the door of his room, he saw that the lamp on the bedside table was burning again, but now its glow revealed nothing except an empty bed. Longarm saw no sign of Natalie.

He frowned, but he wasn't overly worried yet. She had probably gone back to her own room, he told himself, just in case Boulware or someone else came upstairs. She didn't want to be found in Longarm's room—or in his bed. Despite the wanton way she had behaved tonight, she probably still worried enough about propriety to prompt that move. So he left his door open, stepped across the hall, and knocked softly on the door of the room that had been prepared for Natalie.

There was no response.

Longarm's frown deepened. He leaned closer to the door and called softly through it, "Miss Stoneham? Natalie?"

Again, no one answered him.

Now he *was* worried. He reached down, grasped the knob, and twisted it. It turned in his hand. The door was unlocked. He swung it open and stepped inside quickly, gun in hand. The light from his room spilled across the hall and through the open door into Natalie's room.

Longarm's mouth tightened into a grim line as he saw that the bed was empty.

Natalie was gone.

Chapter 11

Longarm struck a match and lit the lamp to be sure, but the yellow glow revealed what he'd been afraid of. Natalie wasn't here, and judging by the unrumpled condition of the bed, she hadn't been all night long. So much for the idea of her moving over here after he had left her in his room.

He swung around with a curse. While he was out prowling around the village, somebody had gotten in here and grabbed Natalie. It was the only answer that made any sense.

Boulware looked up in alarm from his book as Longarm clattered down the stairs. "M'sieu Long!" he exclaimed. "What is wrong?"

"Miss Stoneham's gone!"

Boulware dropped his book and jerked up out of the chair. "*Mon dieu!* You are sure?"

"She's not in her room."

Boulware headed for the stairs. "We should check the other rooms. Perhaps she stepped out, got confused, and went back to a different room. In these old houses, it is easy to get lost."

The house wasn't so big Longarm thought that was likely. Besides, he had told Natalie to stay where she was.

He and Boulware quickly looked in the other rooms on the second floor and still found no sign of Natalie. Longarm asked, "Does your maid or any of the other servants sleep here at night?"

Boulware shook his head. "No, they all have their own homes to which they return. You and I and Miss Stoneham were alone in the house, as far as I know."

Longarm said, "I want to borrow that lantern so I can take a look around outside."

"Of course. Come with me."

Boulware got the lantern for Longarm and then went with him outside. They searched all around the house. Longarm found some fresh bootprints near the back door. They were deep, but the impressions were uniform.

Longarm frowned as he let the lantern light spill over the prints. "These weren't made by the limping man. You can see how the gait is different from his. But whoever left them was either a big man, or carrying a weight, or both."

"Miss Stoneham," said Boulware.

Longarm nodded. "That'd be my guess. He got inside and overpowered her some way, then carried her out. She was probably unconscious, or we would have heard her yelling."

"This is terrible," muttered Boulware. "Who could it have been?"

"Somebody working with the limping man, maybe. He distracted us while the other fella did the dirty work and kidnapped Natalie . . . Miss Stoneham."

"The limping man has always been alone when he was seen around here. . . ."

"But that doesn't mean he couldn't have a partner," Longarm pointed out.

"No, of course not." Boulware gestured at the prints on the ground. "Can you follow these tracks?"

"I'm sure as hell gonna try."

Longarm was able to follow the tracks by using the

lantern, but they just looped around through the trees that lined Bayou Noir and then stopped where a horse had been left. The fresh droppings told Longarm that much.

"He had a horse tied up here, whoever he was," Longarm said to Boulware. "He put Natalie over the back of the animal, mounted up, and rode away. Let's see if we can tell which way he went. . . ."

The hoofprints led to the main trail that ran parallel to the twisting course of Bayou Noir. Although the prints soon disappeared on the hardpacked surface, Longarm was able to tell that the rider had started north.

"Another sign pointing to Coffin Hill," he said.

"I told you that was an evil place, m'sieu. I believe it now more than ever."

"Yeah, well, now I've got one more reason to go up there."

"You don't intend to go tonight!" Boulware sounded alarmed.

Longarm shook his head. "No, I'd be running too much risk of losing the trail. Whoever grabbed Miss Stoneham could leave the road somewhere along the way, before reaching the plantation. I might miss that at night. Waiting bothers the hell out of me, but I think it'd be best if I rode up there in the morning."

"I agree," said Boulware. "Besides, dawn isn't that far away, only a few hours. You should get some more rest and make a fresh start in the morning."

Longarm nodded, but with Natalie in the hands of whoever the hell had grabbed her, he wasn't sure he would be able to sleep any more tonight.

His hunch was right. He was restless and was never able to fully doze off the rest of the night. He gave up trying when the smell of coffee drifted upstairs and told him that breakfast was being prepared below.

The sky outside was gray with the approach of dawn as

Longarm and Boulware ate in the kitchen of the old house. The Frenchman's cook was the same mulatto woman who served as his maid. She dished up a good breakfast, including cups of strong coffee flavored with chicory, as was common in Louisiana. Longarm was still extremely worried about Natalie, but he stoked up on grits and ham and coffee anyway, since he didn't know how long this day was going to last.

By the time he stepped out of the house onto the front porch, Davey was waiting with the bay, which had been saddled and cared for. The young man said, "Bullroar tells me the lady is missin'. You want me to come with you to help you look for her, Mr. Long?"

Longarm summoned up a weary grin. "You can't fool me, old son. You just want to go up to Coffin Hill and raise a little hell, maybe get a shot at the limping man."

"I reckon it's my duty," said Davey with a shrug. "What if the lady was taken because the limpin' man couldn't get me?"

Boulware followed Longarm onto the porch, a cup of coffee in his hand. He said, "You have responsibilities here, Davey."

"M'sieu Boulware is right," agreed Longarm. "You'd best stay here, at least for now. If I find that I need help, I'll try to get word to you folks here in Pont-a-Mousson."

"We will stand ready to come to your aid if you need us," promised Boulware. Somewhat reluctantly, Davey went along with that.

Longarm swung up into the saddle and said, "All I have to do to find Coffin Hill is follow the trail along the bayou?"

"That will get you there, *mon ami*," said Boulware. "But surely you do not intend to ride in openly?"

"If the folks who live there are mixed up in the bad things going on around here, they've probably figured out already that I'll be coming to see them. Maybe if I just

110

ride in like I don't suspect them, it'll throw them a mite off balance."

"A risky plan," said Boulware with a note of caution in his voice.

"I reckon so, but I'm willing to run a few risks if it gets Natalie back and helps get to the bottom of all this." Longarm lifted a hand to the brim of his Stetson, gave Boulware and Davey a nod, then turned the horse and sent it loping northward along the bayou trail. Within moments, the twists and turns of the dark stream had caused Pont-a-Mousson to fall out of sight behind him.

As the sun rose higher, the green light in the tunnel-like trail brightened somewhat, but it was still gloomy and oppressive here along the bayou. Longarm wasn't sure why anybody would want to live here—but the folks who did probably felt the same way about the part of the country he was from.

Worry over Natalie gnawed at his guts. He told himself that he never should have left her alone. But at the time he had been going out to see what all the yelling was about. He had thought that the danger was outside Boulware's house, rather than inside.

That worry stayed with him over the next couple of hours as he rode toward Coffin Hill. His mood wasn't improved by the swamp that closed in on the other side of the trail from the bayou. The road had been built up here to get it out of the water that glistened blackly between the huge roots of mangrove and cypress trees. The tree limbs were hung with Spanish moss. Even though the air was dead still in here, when Longarm looked at the moss for too long, it seemed to start moving, like thin, skeletal fingers waving and beckoning to him. He grimaced as that thought went through his head.

Eventually the swamp receded and the land on both sides of the bayou rose to form fields. Longarm saw signs that those fields had been cultivated in the past, although they weren't being worked now. Then as he rode around a bend in the trail, he spotted the first people he had seen since leaving Pont-a-Mousson. A row of workers with hoes in their hands labored on the far side of a field, about three hundred yards away. That was too far for Longarm to make out any details about them.

He saw a man sitting on a horse, though, with a rifle held across the saddle in front of him.

Like a guard watching a chain gang full of prisoners.

That thought brought a frown to Longarm's face as he pushed on toward Coffin Hill. Boulware had said that all of the plantation's slaves had left as soon as they were freed. Tristam Blanchard, the master of Coffin Hill, must have hired workers to replace them, otherwise he wouldn't have been able to keep the place going.

A few minutes later, Longarm came in sight of the plantation house itself. From a distance it was a huge mansion gleaming with whitewash, sitting atop a low knoll that made it look even more imposing. The elevation wasn't much, but Longarm supposed that it qualified as a hill to flatlanders who had been raised in these parts. Large white columns supported a roof that jutted out over the gallery along the front of the house.

A tree-lined lane led from the bayou trail up to the plantation house. Beyond the mansion were a barn, a smokehouse, shanties that had once housed slaves, and other outbuildings. Longarm supposed the current workers lived in the old slave quarters.

As he came closer, he could tell that, much like Boulware's house, Coffin Hill showed some signs of age and disrepair. It hadn't been kept up as well as it might have been.

He followed the lane to the front of the house and dismounted there. A hitching post stood beside a gravel walk. He tied the bay's reins to it and went to the large, impressive front door. A lion's-head knocker was in the center of it. Longarm grasped the ring and rapped twice, sharply.

The alacrity with which the door was opened told him that the inhabitants of the house had seen him coming. He expected a servant to greet him, but instead a young woman in a fine gown stood there, a smile on her face.

"Good morning," she said. "Welcome to Coffin Hill, sir. What can we do for you?"

"I'm looking for a fella named Blanchard," replied Longarm as he touched the brim of his hat, figuring there was no point in beating around the bush.

"That would be my father," said the young woman. "Please, won't you come in?"

She moved back to usher him into the house. He stepped into a well-appointed foyer with a highly polished hardwood floor.

The young woman was very attractive, with a dark, somewhat exotic look about her. Raven-black hair tumbled thickly to her shoulders, which were left partially bare by the low-cut neckline of her gown. She was petite, at least a full head shorter than Longarm, but the curves of her body in the tight gown made it abundantly clear she was a grown woman. Her eyes were dark and striking in a sensuously attractive face.

"Might I inquire as to your name, sir?" she asked as she closed the door behind Longarm.

"Custis Long, ma'am."

"I'm Cecilia Blanchard."

Longarm took off his hat and gave her a polite nod. "Pleased to meet you, ma'am."

"Do you have business with my father, Mr. Long?"

"Well, I don't rightly know. I'd like to ask him a few questions and discuss a matter with him."

She smiled again, dimpling prettily. "He's in the library. Won't you come with me?"

"Much obliged, ma'am." Still holding his hat, Longarm followed her down a hallway to a set of double doors. She opened them and preceded him into the room.

"Father, you have a visitor," Cecilia Blanchard announced. "Mr. Custis Long."

"Custis . . . That's a fine old Southern name." A man seated behind a desk stood up and came around it with his hand extended as Longarm entered the room. "I'm very pleased to meet you, sir. What brings you to Coffin Hill?"

Tristam Blanchard was a medium-sized man with graying, thinning brown hair and a mustache that drooped over a wide mouth. Longarm pegged his age at almost sixty, which meant that Cecilia must have been born rather late to Blanchard and his wife.

"I'm looking for someone," Longarm replied bluntly as he shook hands with Blanchard. "Two somebodies, actually. A young fella named Matthew Chadwick and his cousin Miss Natalie Stoneham."

Blanchard frowned as if he were utterly baffled. "And you have reason to believe that these folks are here, Mr. Long? I hate to disappoint you, but I've never heard of either of them." He looked at his daughter. "What about you, Cecilia?"

She shook her head. "I'm afraid not."

Longarm didn't believe either one of them. He couldn't have said *why* he doubted what they had just told him, but he did.

But accusing them of outright lying probably wouldn't get him anywhere, so he said, "Mr. Chadwick was reported to have been in this area several weeks ago. Miss Stoneham and I were searching for him when we got separated. I know she'd planned to come on up Bayou Noir to your plantation, so I was hoping I'd find her here."

"I'm truly sorry. I'll tell you what, Mr. Long, I'll summon my overseer." Blanchard chuckled. "Sometimes I think he knows more about what's going on around here than I do." Speaking again to his daughter, he went on, "Cecilia, darlin', will you have one of the boys run down to the fields and fetch Hank?"

"Of course," murmured the young woman. She left the library.

Blanchard waved Longarm into a leather armchair in front of the desk. "While we're waiting for Hank, why don't you have a seat, Mr. Long? Cigar? Or a drink, even though it's a mite early in the day?"

"No, thanks," said Longarm as he sat down. "If the folks I'm looking for aren't here, I reckon I'll have to be moving on."

Blanchard frowned as he settled himself in the chair behind the desk. "I'm sorry, Mr. Long, but this is what you'd call the end of the line, I guess. There's nothin' north of here for miles except swampland, and I hardly think it's likely that two strangers would be up there. If they are, they're surely unlucky, because the swamp is no place for folks who don't know what they're doing."

"I expect you're right about that," said Longarm with a nod. He didn't have to work very hard to put a worried look on his face. "I just don't know what could have happened to them."

"Well, maybe Hank can help," Blanchard said.

Longarm glanced around the room while they were waiting. The only window was behind Blanchard's desk. The rest of the wall space was taken up by shelves filled with thick volumes bound in dark leather. Longarm noticed several sets of law books.

Blanchard saw where he was looking and smiled. "At one time in my life I read for the law," he explained, "but taking care of the plantation prevented me from pursuing a legal career. And then the war came along . . ." He stopped and made a sour face. "Then the war came along and ruined everything."

Not if you were a slave, thought Longarm, but he kept

that comment to himself, knowing that Blanchard wouldn't take it kindly. Even though he didn't trust the man, he didn't want to give Blanchard an excuse to have him thrown off the place.

A few minutes later the door of the library opened again, and a big man strode into the room. As Longarm stood up and turned to face him, he saw that the newcomer was as tall as he was and as broad in the shoulders. He had a craggy, beard-stubbled face under the floppy brim of a felt hat. At his waist a coiled bullwhip hung on his belt. Longarm had a strong hunch this was the man he had seen sitting on horseback and watching the workers in the field he had passed earlier.

Blanchard got to his feet behind the desk and said, "Mr. Long, this is Hank Hennigan, my overseer."

Overseer, noted Longarm, not "foreman" or "ramrod" or anything like that. Blanchard used a term that went all the way back to slave days. Hennigan looked like he would have been right at home back in that time, too.

Hennigan grunted and gave Longarm a nod, but he didn't offer to shake hands, which was all right with the big lawman. He disliked Hennigan on sight.

"What's this about, boss?" asked Hennigan in a deep, guttural voice.

"Mr. Long is looking for a couple of folks. I don't recall their names. . . ."

"Matthew Chadwick and Miss Natalie Stoneham," supplied Longarm.

Hennigan shook his head. "Never heard of 'em."

"Maybe you've seen some strangers around here lately—"

"No strangers at Coffin Hill," Hennigan broke in. "If there was, I'd know about it. Ain't nothin' happens on this plantation without me knowin' about it."

"That's what makes you such a fine overseer, Hank,"

said Blanchard. "I suppose you can head back to the fields now—"

"Wait just a minute," said Longarm. "What about a fella with a bad limp? Either of you seen anybody like that around here?"

The looks of surprise on their faces seemed to be genuine. Hennigan stepped closer to Longarm. His mouth quirked angrily as he asked, "What the hell do you know about that limpin' son of a bitch, mister?"

Chapter 12

"Hank!" Blanchard said before Longarm could reply to Hennigan's question. "Remember that Mr. Long is our guest."

"Yeah," Hennigan said sullenly. "I reckon. But if he knows something about the limpin' man, he needs to tell us."

Longarm shook his head. "I don't know a blessed thing, old son, except that I've seen the hombre a time or two . . . and bad things seem to happen whenever he's around."

Hennigan grunted again. "Damn right they do. That's why I'd like to get my hands on him."

Longarm's thoughts were spinning crazily now. As much as he had believed earlier that Blanchard and Hennigan were lying about knowing the whereabouts of Natalie and the fate of Matthew Chadwick, he believed they were genuinely mystified by the limping man. Longarm's theory had been that the master of Coffin Hill was up to no good and that the limping man was connected with him somehow. Now it looked like that part of the speculation, at least, was wrong.

Blanchard leaned forward and rested his hands on the desk. "Where did you see this limping man, Mr. Long?"

Longarm didn't see any harm in telling the truth about

this. "The first time was a couple of days ago on the trail into Saint Angelique. The second was yesterday on the trail between there and here. The other times I didn't actually see him myself, but other folks did. I just missed him. Two nights ago he was spotted in Saint Angelique, near the shack of a man who got his throat cut, and last night he was seen in a little settlement down the bayou called Pont-a-Mousson."

"I'm familiar with it," said Blanchard, and from the sound of his voice he wasn't too fond of the community founded by Andres Boulware. "What happened there?"

"That's where I got separated from Miss Stoneham," said Longarm. "The folks who live there seem to think the limping man got her."

"Probably did." That comment came from Hennigan. "I think the bastard's some sort o' haint."

"He's no ghost," said Longarm. "He left prints. I saw them with my own eyes."

Blanchard straightened and nodded. "I apologize if we seemed abrupt, Mr. Long. It's just that this man has been skulkin' around the area for quite some time, and no one seems to know who he is or what he wants here. The mystery has made us all a mite nervous."

"Reckon I can understand that. Sorry I can't help you."

Blanchard waved a hand. "The best thing for you to do might be to return to Saint Angelique and turn the matter of your missing friends over to Sheriff Duquesne. He's a highly competent lawman."

"I'll think about it," Longarm said, even though he didn't trust Duquesne any more than he trusted Blanchard and Hennigan.

"In the meantime, you'll stay and share the noon meal with us, I suppose?"

"Well, I don't know . . ."

"Please, sir, we get so few visitors up here. I'm sure Cecilia would be very happy to have a guest for a while."

Longarm intended to poke around Coffin Hill some

more before he left, so the invitation played right into his hands. He nodded and said, "I appreciate the hospitality, Mr. Blanchard."

"You're quite welcome. I'll tell Cecilia to inform the cook that we'll have one more for dinner. Hank, you can return to work now."

Hennigan nodded curtly and left the room. Blanchard led Longarm out as well, saying, "We'll go to the parlor where we can be more comfortable."

When they came into the parlor, Cecilia Blanchard turned away from the window where she had been standing and looking out at a garden so overgrown with large, drooping flowers that it resembled a jungle. She smiled at Longarm and said, "I'm sorry you didn't have any luck finding the people you're looking for, Mr. Long."

Blanchard said, "On the good side, my dear, Mr. Long has agreed to sit down to dinner with us and visit for a while."

Cecilia clapped her hands together lightly. "Oh, good! We get so few visitors here at Coffin Hill."

Blanchard had said just about the same thing, and his prediction that Cecilia would be happy was proven true as she came over to Longarm, linked her arm with his, and led him back to the window.

"Aren't the flowers lovely?" she said. "They're my pride and joy."

Blanchard beamed proudly and said, "Cecilia is *my* pride and joy. She has been the lady of the house since her poor mother passed on a few years ago. Whatever brightness can be found here is her doin'."

Cecilia laughed. "My father is too kind, Mr. Long. He's the master of Coffin Hill, the one responsible for everything that goes on here."

Longarm wasn't sure what to make of that comment, but he was aware that Cecilia Blanchard was leaning against him, and she had to know that her breast was prodding softly on his arm as she did so. She looked up at him from her diminutive height and smiled. The sparkle in her dark eyes managed to be both mischievous and sensuous at the same time.

"Could I interest you in a cigar, Mr. Long?" asked Blanchard. "I have some fine ones from Havana."

Longarm turned to him and said, "I generally smoke three-for-a-nickel cheroots. Reckon it wouldn't hurt to try something else for a change."

Blanchard chuckled again. "Then you're in for a treat, my friend." He reached in his coat pocket and took out a couple of cigars. Longarm struck a match and lit both of them, and soon the air in the parlor was hazed with blue, aromatic smoke.

If the circumstances had been different, Longarm might have enjoyed visiting with Tristam Blanchard and his daughter. Blanchard seemed to be a well-educated man, and like most Southern gentlemen he was a talker, ready, willing, and able to discourse at length on a variety of subjects.

And Cecilia was certainly beautiful, pleasant company. As Longarm looked at her smiling face, he wondered if she was aware of whatever her father was up to or if he was carrying on some sort of malignant scheme without her knowing about it. She *looked* innocent enough—but Longarm knew from experience that such considerations usually meant little or nothing.

A young black man came into the parlor and reported, "I done took care o' the gentleman's horse, suh, like Massa Hennigan tol' me to."

"Thank you, Lucius," said Blanchard. As the boy nodded and went out, the plantation owner turned to Longarm and went on, "I suppose Hank decided that since you'll be staying for a while, your mount should have some grain and water."

"I appreciate that," said Longarm, even though it would have been fine with him if everybody had kept their hands

122

off the bay. He didn't plan on staying at Coffin Hill for all that long. . . .

But he would be back under cover of darkness, he thought. He was convinced that the key to the disappearances of Chadwick and Natalie was here. There was no other place they could have gone from Pont-a-Mousson.

A maid entered the parlor a short time later and said that dinner was ready. She was a young black woman, and at the sight of her, Longarm had the same thought that had crossed his mind when the young man came in. All the slaves might have left Coffin Hill after they were freed, as Boulware had said, but obviously some black people had returned to work on the plantation, probably ones who had not been held here in servitude before the war. Folks had to make a living somehow.

Cecilia linked her arm with Longarm's again as they walked to the dining room. Like everywhere else he'd been in the South, the glories of antebellum life were still visible in the big room, but they were starting to fade and fray around the edges.

Blanchard sat at the head of the long table, with Cecilia on his right hand and Longarm across the table on his left. The food was good, starting with a spicy gumbo and proceeding to fried chicken with all the fixins. Longarm didn't really pay that much attention to what he was eating, though. Most of his attention was devoted to Blanchard's conversation. He hoped the plantation owner would drop some inadvertent hint as to what was going on around here. However, that didn't happen.

When the meal was over, Longarm said, "I'm much obliged to you folks for your hospitality, but I reckon it's time for me to be moving on."

"You're going back to Saint Angelique?" asked Blanchard.

"Don't see as I have much choice. You said there's nothing past here but swamp."

A little shudder ran through Cecilia's body. "I hate the swamp," she said. "It's so dark and dismal. Terrible things could happen in there, and no one would ever know it."

Blanchard sipped from a glass of wine and said, "Terrible things can happen anywhere, darlin'. Light or dark, all closed up or out in the open, middle of the night or straight-up noon. When evil strikes, it shows no respect for places or persons. Don't you agree, Mr. Long?"

Longarm nodded. "I reckon so. Bad things usually come at you with not much warning. But I've got to say that I agree with Miss Blanchard, too. I don't much like the swamp, either."

She smiled across the table at him and said, "Please, call me Cecilia. And do you really have to go? We get so little company up here."

"Sorry," said Longarm.

"Go see Remy Duquesne when you get back to Saint Angelique," said Blanchard. "He'll get to the bottom of this, don't you worry."

Longarm got to his feet. "I'm obliged for the advice, too," he said, even though he didn't intend to follow it.

Cecilia gave Longarm a sad, wistful smile but didn't follow him onto the porch. Blanchard did. One of the young grooms came running, and the plantation owner ordered, "Bring up Mr. Long's horse."

The servant hustled off to the barn. As Longarm looked around the place, he thought that it was almost like he had been transported back in time twenty-five or thirty years. The workers in the fields, the hard-faced overseer, the plantation house . . . all of it was reminiscent of things he had read in that book by Mrs. Stowe. Of course, her novel had contained a lot of melodrama, exaggerations, and outright falsehoods, but some of it had a basis in fact, too.

"Massa Blanchard!" the groom called as he led the bay out of the barn. "Looks like this fella's hoss gone lame."

"What!" exclaimed Longarm. He felt a surge of surprise and anger as he saw that the horse was limping on one of its rear legs. He hurried down the steps from the porch.

"Picked up a stone, maybe," suggested Blanchard as he followed.

Longarm went around the horse and carefully lifted the bad leg. He took out his folding knife and used the blade to pry under the shoe. Sure enough, after a moment he dislodged a small pebble. The area of the hoof where it had been wedged was sore.

Blanchard nodded sagely. "That's what I thought. Bad luck that it happened, Custis—you don't mind if I call you Custis, do you?—but good luck for you that the animal went lame here, instead of out on the trail. Give him a day or two of rest and he'll be good as new, I'll wager."

Longarm let the horse's leg down, straightened, and rasped a thumbnail along his jaw. "Yeah," he said. "Have you got a mount I could borrow?"

"I'm afraid not. But we have plenty of room in the house, and you're more than welcome to stay while your horse recovers." Blanchard smiled. "I know that will make Cecilia happy."

Longarm's brain was working furiously. Although it wasn't impossible, he didn't believe that the bay had picked up the stone in its shoe on the ride up here from Pont-a-Mousson. There just weren't that many rocks to be found along the bayou trail. Nor had the horse shown any signs of going lame during the morning.

But if somebody had *put* that stone in the horseshoe on purpose and then led the bay around all the time that Longarm had been inside the plantation house, that would have resulted in the horse being unable to travel.

Which would mean that somebody didn't want him to leave Coffin Hill.

Blanchard hadn't ordered that a trick like that be carried out, because Longarm had been with him the whole time.

125

But Hank Hennigan could have. The overseer had taken no pains to conceal the fact that he didn't like Longarm. If Hennigan was responsible, had he done it out of sheer maliciousness, or did he have some other reason?

The only way to find out was to play along with the scheme.

Those thoughts went through Longarm's mind in a matter of a couple of heartbeats. Now he nodded and said, "Well, it looks like I'm obliged to you again, Mr. Blanchard. I'll accept your kind offer."

"I'm glad to hear it." Blanchard held out a hand. "Come on back inside and we'll tell Cecilia that you're staying." As he ushered Longarm into the house, Blanchard added over his shoulder to the groom, "See that Mr. Long's horse is properly taken care of."

Somebody had already taken care of it, thought Longarm. Taken care of things so well that he was stuck here on this plantation, where danger might well lurk behind its genteel façade.

Cecilia practically squealed in glee when she learned that Longarm would be staying at Coffin Hill for a day or two. She had to be really starved for company, he thought—or else she was acting and putting on a good show. He hadn't quite decided which yet.

She insisted on giving him a guided tour of the plantation, which really didn't take all that long, and then Longarm spent the rest of the afternoon in the library with Blanchard, smoking Cuban cigars and drinking brandy. Cecilia sat quietly with them, evidently absorbed by every word of their conversation. Something about her intent attitude struck Longarm as odd. He supposed it was possible that a young, vivacious girl like her would simply be happy to have a visitor in the house.

Supper that evening was just as tasty as the midday

meal had been. Afterward, they went into the parlor again. Longarm had noticed a small piano there earlier in the day, so he wasn't surprised when Cecilia played for them. She had a good touch with the instrument, producing lilting melodies that made her father smile with pride.

"Cecilia had lessons in New Orleans," said Blanchard, "but she also has a natural talent."

"Mighty pretty," said Longarm. "And her piano playing's not bad, either."

That brought a pleased laugh from Cecilia.

The evening was so pleasant that Longarm had to remind himself he was smack-dab in the middle of a hotbed of intrigue and potential danger. Blanchard could be responsible for Natalie's disappearance, as well as that of Matthew Chadwick.

On the other hand, the question of the limping man still haunted him. Maybe he had misjudged Blanchard, and so had Andres Boulware. The limping man might be responsible for all the deviltry going on around here.

Well, not *all* of it, amended Longarm. The limping man hadn't put that stone in the bay's shoe. Somebody from Coffin Hill had done that. He was convinced of it.

When it came time to retire for the evening, Blanchard said, "I had one of the maids prepare our best guest room for you, Custis. I'll take you up and show it to you."

"Mighty kind of you," said Longarm.

He clasped Cecilia's hand for a moment when she offered it to him, and she surprised him by coming up on her toes and brushing a kiss across his cheek. Blanchard saw the gesture but didn't seem to mind.

"Good night, Custis," Cecilia murmured. "I hope you sleep well."

He was going to sleep with one eye open, that was for sure—although he didn't tell them that.

Blanchard took him upstairs to the guest room. It was

comfortably furnished with a four-poster bed, a couple of wicker armchairs, a fine mahogany chifforobe, and a woven rug on the floor next to the bed.

"You should be comfortable here," Blanchard said.

Longarm nodded. "I'm sure I will be."

"Good night, then."

"Good night, Mr. Blanchard . . . and thanks again for your hospitality."

"Think nothing of it," said Blanchard as he went out.

Longarm saw that his bag had been placed in the room, but not his Winchester. The fact that his rifle was probably still out in the barn didn't *have* to mean anything—but it was one more subtle indication that not everything might be as it seemed at Coffin Hill.

He undressed down to the bottoms of his long underwear, placed his coiled gun belt and holstered Colt on a bedside table, and climbed into the four-poster. The straw mattress was a little softer than he liked, but he supposed he could live with it. He didn't blow out the lamp yet because he wanted to think over everything that had happened. Too many unanswered questions still plagued him.

He hadn't solved any of the mysteries facing him by the time a floorboard creaked softly just outside his door. The warning sound wasn't much, but it was enough to put Longarm instantly on the alert. The door didn't have a lock, and he hadn't wedged a chair under the knob. He had a hunch he was going to have a visitor, or visitors, before the night was over, and he was ready for them. His hand closed over the butt of the Colt and slipped the revolver out of its holster.

The knob turned and the door opened slowly at first, then quickly. A slight figure slid through the opening and eased the door shut.

Cecilia Blanchard gasped as she turned to face the bed and saw Longarm sitting there with a gun in his hand. The barrel was pointed right at her.

"Custis!" she said. "What are you doing?"

"Habit," he said. "I'm used to being careful."

He had figured that one of three people would come through that door, so he wasn't all that surprised to see Cecilia. The question now was—why was she here?

And what was he going to learn from her?

She wore a blue silk robe that clung to her body. Her dark hair was loose around her shoulders, and she looked incredibly lovely. Longarm lowered the gun as she came closer to the bed and put out her hands toward him, imploringly.

"Custis," she said in a low, urgent voice, "I have a . . . a tremendous favor to ask of you. You have to help me get out of here. You have to take me with you when you go."

"And why would I do that?" asked Longarm.

Cecilia's hands went to the knotted strip of silk around her waist and tugged it free. The robe parted, revealing smooth skin with just a hint of an olive hue beneath it. A shrug of Cecilia's shoulders sent the garment sliding off them. It dropped to the floor around her feet, revealing that her small but perfectly shaped body was nude underneath it.

"I can make it worth your while," she said. "Like my father told you, I have a natural talent, Custis. And it's not just for playing the piano."

Chapter 13

The offer didn't surprise Longarm, either. The question now was whether or not he was going to take her up on it.

"Not that I don't appreciate it, Cecilia, but why are you doing this?" he asked. "Why do you want to get away from here so bad that you'd come to the bed of a fella you've only known for a few hours?"

"Well, it's not *just* that," she said as she came closer to the bed, her hips swaying a little. "I find you a very attractive man. I probably shouldn't admit it, but I wanted you as soon as I saw you."

"But what's wrong that makes you want to leave?" he persisted.

She lowered a hip to the edge of the bed and perched there. As she leaned toward him, she asked in a throaty voice, "Wouldn't you rather talk about this *after* we've made love?"

One of her pert little breasts was within easy reach of his hand. He cupped it and ran his thumb over the hard nipple in its brown ring. Cecilia sighed with pleasure.

"I reckon your pa would be mighty upset with me if I was to run off with you," said Longarm. "He might set the law on me and claim I kidnapped you. I'd have to have a really good reason to risk that."

She caught hold of his hand with both of hers and lowered it from her breast to the small triangle of dark hair between her legs. As she pressed her pelvis to his palm, she asked, "Isn't this a good enough reason?"

His middle finger dipped down to the fleshy folds at her opening and found them already damp. He slipped his finger inside her, which made her close her eyes and breathe another long sigh. He felt the smooth, buttery muscles tighten on his finger.

"Please, Custis," she whispered. "Just make love to me now. I'll tell you everything after we're done, I promise."

"Swear to it?" he asked, even though he was aroused now, too, and was having a difficult time keeping his mind on anything except how tight and hot her femininity was.

"I . . . I swear!" she gasped as her hips began to pump and her sex clasped his finger even more urgently.

Before either of them could say anything else, Cecilia threw herself against Longarm and wrapped her arms around his neck as she pressed her mouth to his. Her sudden movement dislodged his finger from her, but she didn't seem to care. She was too caught up in the moment and the passionate kiss they were sharing. Her tongue insinuated itself into Longarm's mouth.

She tasted mighty sweet. Longarm's tongue circled and swooped, doing sensuous battle with hers. As she straddled his hips he slid his hands down her sleek back to the swell of her rump. He filled each hand with a firm, rounded cheek and used that grip to pull her more tightly against him. She rubbed her groin on the hard prod of his erect manhood, which was still trapped inside the long underwear.

Cecilia broke the kiss, tossed her hair back, and said breathlessly, "Let's get that thing out of there and into me!"

She slid back a little so that she could reach down and grasp the waistband of his underwear. As he lifted his hips, she pulled the garment over them, freeing his shaft so that it sprang up and almost hit her in the face.

"Good Lord, Custis! Be careful. You could kill somebody with that club!"

"Never have yet," he said.

She giggled, reminding him of just how young she was. Not inexperienced, though. Clearly she was no blushing virgin. The way she wrapped both hands around him and commenced to pumping was proof of that. It was Longarm's turn to give a low, throaty moan of pleasure.

She didn't keep up the stroking for very long. "Don't want to waste this," she said as she lifted herself again and poised her hips over his. "I'm not sure I can take all of it, but I'm going to try."

"Go at it slow and easy," advised Longarm.

"Just not *too* slow or *too* easy, right?" Cecilia smiled as she began to lower herself onto him.

It felt wonderful when the tip of his shaft touched the hot, wet opening of her body. The lips spread around the crown as she took in a couple of inches. She lowered herself another inch, and a worried look appeared on her face.

"It's so thick," she whispered, "and I'm small."

"Careful now," said Longarm as he grasped her hips to steady her. "A little bit at a time."

Biting gently at her lower lip, Cecilia slowly sank down to sheath even more of him inside her. She said, "Ahhhh," a few times, and closed her eyes and rolled her head from side to side. The look of trepidation was soon replaced by one of excitement and ecstasy as she stretched inside to accommodate him.

It took several minutes, but she finally hit bottom. Every bit of his shaft was buried inside her. And judging from the expression on her face it was one of the most glorious feelings she had ever experienced.

It was pretty damned good for Longarm, too. The heat was incredible. She was so tight he wasn't sure he would be able to move any, but that didn't really matter. It felt plenty exciting just being inside her like this.

Slowly, Cecilia began to rock her hips back and forth as she rode on Longarm's cock. That created some friction and seemed to make her even wetter. "I'm getting used to it now," she said with her eyes closed and a blissful expression on her beautiful face. "It feels so wonderful. Oh, Custis . . ."

Her hips pumped harder. Longarm filled his hands with her breasts and squeezed them. Cecilia panted from the excitement that was growing within her. Longarm felt his own arousal swelling higher and higher.

Within moments she was jerking and thrusting like she was atop a galloping steed. Longarm dropped his hands to her hips again and braced her. Cecilia gasped, "Oh! . . . Oh! . . . Oh!" every time he drove into her and reached her utmost depths. After a few minutes, shudders of culmination began to roll through her.

That was enough to set off Longarm's climax, as well. He buried himself as far inside her as he could go and let loose with spurt after spurt of white-hot seed. Cecilia's dark hair flew around her head as she jerked it back and forth from the intensity of her climax.

As the last of Longarm's juices welled out of him into her drenched cavern, Cecilia went limp and sprawled forward onto his broad chest, which was matted with thick, dark brown hair. He felt her heart beating wildly as she lay there on top of him. He stroked her back and her flanks and her hips as he tried to catch his own breath. For the second night in a row, he had made love to a beautiful young woman, and that was something he never grew tired of.

He wasn't completely carried away by the deliciousness of the situation, though. A part of his brain was still alert and still thinking. He hadn't forgotten what had brought him to Coffin Hill. As Cecilia nuzzled his neck, he ran his fingers through her hair, kissed her ear, and then whispered in it, "You were going to tell me why you want to get away from here so much."

She lifted her head, blinked, and looked confused. "What? What did you say?"

"You were going to tell me why you want to get away from here," repeated Longarm. "Is it your father? Does he mistreat you?"

"My father . . ." Cecilia lifted a hand to push her sweat-damp hair out of her face and then said with a savage, surprising intensity, "My father is a damned lunatic!"

She rolled off him and turned so that she was sitting with her back to him. Longarm sat up, too, and put a hand on her shoulder. He could feel her trembling.

"Tell me about it," he said. "If I'm going to help you, I have to know what's going on here."

"He's a madman," she said quietly. "Isn't that enough for you to know?"

"No," said Longarm, "it's not."

Cecilia turned so that she could look at him again. "All right. He never got over the war. He hated the Yankees so much, and believed in slavery so much, that when the war was over and all the slaves had left, he swore that things wouldn't change, not at Coffin Hill. He was going to keep on like he always had."

"But he couldn't," said Longarm. "All the slaves were gone."

Cecilia gave a bitter laugh. "He got more."

"Wait a minute." Longarm leaned toward her. "The folks I saw working in the fields on my way here . . . ?"

"They're not here by choice," she said. "Oh, sure, some of them came to Coffin Hill thinking they would just work on the plantation and be paid wages or shares, but once they got here they found out that my father didn't intend to ever let them leave. And he doesn't pay them, either. He just gives them a place to live and a little food and works them half to death in exchange."

Longarm shook his head in disbelief. "Why don't they just light a shuck out of here?"

"You mean run away? If they tried to do that, they wouldn't live long enough to enjoy their freedom. Hank and the other overseers would see to that."

"There are others besides Hennigan?"

"A dozen or more men. I'm not really sure how many. They stay out of sight for the most part, but they're always around, whether you can see them or not. And they're all armed with rifles and are crack shots. The workers all know that if they tried to run off, they'd be shot down like dogs. They've seen it happen in the past, and all it takes is seeing that a few times to make you realize it's not worth it."

Personally, Longarm couldn't understand that attitude. To him, taking a chance on freedom was always better than living in sure slavery, but he knew not everybody felt the same way.

"The servants I've seen didn't look like they were afraid for their lives."

"That's because they all know how they're supposed to act whenever there are strangers around. If they don't pretend to be cheerful and happy to be here, Hank will take his bullwhip to them later." Cecilia clutched at his arm. "You've got to understand, Custis. I was born just a couple of years before the war started, so I don't really remember what it was like before the slaves were freed. But from everything I've read, and from what my father says, he's recreated that sort of life here at Coffin Hill. He's lost in the past, and he's not going to give it up."

"Maybe not without a fight—"

Her grip on his arm tightened. "No. Never. You're only one man. You can't stop him. You can't change things. All you can do is get me away from here."

"How do you figure we'll manage that if your pa has riflemen hidden all over the place?"

"They don't watch *me*. My father has no idea how much

I hate him and want to get away from him. After you leave, I can slip out of the house and circle around to the trail, so that you can meet me after you're out of sight of the place. Your horse is big enough to carry double. We'll get out of here as fast as we can. We'll have to be careful when we go through Saint Angelique, though, so that Sheriff Duquesne doesn't spot us."

Longarm's eyes narrowed. "Duquesne works with your father, doesn't he?"

Cecilia nodded and said, "Father pays him off to look the other way, I guess you could say."

Longarm sat there quietly for a moment, mulling over everything she had told him. Then he said, "You're not telling me all of it."

"What do you mean? I've been honest with you, Custis."

"As far as it goes. But there are people missing around these parts, and I want to know if your pa has anything to do with that. There are the two folks I'm looking for, Miss Stoneham and her cousin, and a dozen or more young people from Pont-a-Mousson. What do you know about them?"

Cecilia gazed down at the bed for a second before lifting her eyes and looking at Longarm again. "It's true," she whispered. "Not enough workers come here voluntarily, so whenever any travelers ride along the bayou trail, they . . . they come to Coffin Hill and they never leave. Father has an arrangement with a man in Saint Angelique named Jacquard, to guide people who want to hunt and fish up here. . . ."

"*Had* an arrangement with Jacquard, you mean," said Longarm. "He's dead. I reckon Duquesne cut his throat."

Cecilia stared at him and asked, "Why would the sheriff do that?"

"Because he knew I was sniffing around, looking for Matthew Chadwick. He knew Chadwick had left Saint Angelique on a trip into the swamps with Jacquard as his guide, and he knew what that meant. So he probably figured your pa wouldn't want me talking to Jacquard and maybe finding out what's been going on up here. So he made sure Jacquard would never talk to anybody again."

Cecilia shivered. "Yes, he might do something like that. He's ruthless enough."

"What about the folks missing from Pont-a-Mousson?" asked Longarm.

"That's Hank's doing." Now that she was confessing, the words spilled eagerly from her. "When we need more workers here on the plantation, Hank goes down to that village and waits for a chance to grab someone. Father hates that Frenchman, Boulware, and all the people who live there. He says that they're all slaves and the children of slaves, so we're really just taking back what rightfully belongs to us."

Longarm felt a cold chill go along his spine at the thought that a man could be as demented as Tristam Blanchard seemed to be. He might have to bring in the army to help him, but one way or another he vowed to clean out this rat's nest.

He wasn't finished with his questions. "These men who work with Hennigan, the other overseers . . . is one of them the limping man?"

Without hesitation, Cecilia shook her head. "I swear, Custis, none of us know anything about the limping man, other than the fact that he's been seen around here and folks seem to be scared of him. I know he makes Hank and my father nervous, because they don't know what he's up to."

Longarm frowned as he scraped a thumbnail along his jawline. The identity of that damned limping man was still elusive.

Something else had been nagging at the back of his brain for the past few minutes, and suddenly he realized what it was. "You said folks who come here are taken prisoner and forced to work as slaves. Does that mean Matthew Chadwick is still alive?"

"I don't know. I honestly don't. I saw him when Hank and the others brought him in, after Jacquard led him into a trap, but he was taken off to the slave quarters and I never caught sight of him after that. He might be alive, but if he fought too much, they might have killed him and thrown his body in the swamp for the gators. That's what they do to anyone whose spirit they can't break." Cecilia paused. "But I do know the woman is here. Miss Stoneham."

This time it was Longarm who gripped her arm tightly. "You're sure?"

She nodded. "Hank went down to Pont-a-Mousson last night and grabbed her. Father got a message from Sheriff Duquesne yesterday that said you and Miss Stoneham were on your way up here. He decided to have Hank kidnap her first, just in case he needed her as a hostage to use against you."

"If your father's heard from Duquesne, then he knows that I'm—"

"A federal marshal?" Cecilia nodded. "Yes, he knows about that, too."

Longarm thought about the stone that had been placed in the bay's shoe to make the horse go lame. "If he knows I'm a lawman, chances are he doesn't plan to let me leave. So I may not be able to help you get away."

"But you *have* to," she said. "All you need to do is pretend that you believe everything he told you. If he doesn't think that you suspect him, he'll let you ride away. He knows that if he kills a federal lawman, or even just keeps you here as a prisoner, your superiors will just send in more men. He doesn't want that kind of attention."

Longarm thought it over and nodded. What she said made sense. So what he had to do now was fool Blanchard into thinking that *he* had been fooled. That was the only chance he and Cecilia had of getting away from here.

But that would mean abandoning Natalie for the time being, until he could get back with a troop of cavalry or a posse of deputy marshals. And there was no telling what might happen to her while he was gone.

"Where's Miss Stoneham being held?" he asked.

"Why?"

"I don't reckon I can just leave her here."

Cecilia clutched at him. "But you can't help her now, Custis! And if you try to, my father will know you've found out the truth about him. Worse, he'll know that someone betrayed him, and he'll figure out it was me!" She shook her head emphatically. "No, if you try to help her, you'll ruin everything for me. Neither of us will ever get away. I can't let you do that, Custis."

"I won't leave without her," he declared, his voice hardening.

She stared at him, and the warmth in her eyes grew cold. "Then you won't leave at all," she said. "Maybe the next marshal to come here looking for you won't be so stubborn."

He made a grab for her, but she was already moving and he missed. She lunged out of bed and practically flew across the room to the door. As she threw it open, she screamed, "Hank! Hank! Help me!"

Longarm bit back a curse and swung his legs out of bed, pulling up his long underwear as he did so. He hadn't counted on Cecilia turning on him so suddenly, just because he didn't want to abandon Natalie.

He made a grab for his gun, but as he pulled it out of the holster and started to turn toward the door, a heavy step sounded. Something cracked almost like a rifle shot and a searing pain burst on the back of his right hand. His fingers jerked open involuntarily. The Colt slipped from his grasp and thudded to the floor.

Hank Hennigan stood in the doorway, the long black bullwhip that hung from his hand writhing and coiling on the floor at his feet almost like it was alive. He had just wielded the whip with deadly accuracy, its weighted tip tearing open a blood-dripping gash in the back of Longarm's hand.

A still naked Cecilia huddled against Hennigan's left side. She said, "Thank God you're here, Hank. He . . . he tore my clothes off and tried to attack me!"

Longarm didn't know whether Hennigan believed her or if it even mattered anymore. The brutal overseer laughed and flicked his wrist so that the whip leaped up and cracked again. He pushed the nude, cowering Cecilia behind him and took a step toward Longarm.

"I'm gonna strip the hide right off of you, you son of a bitch," he said, "and I'm gonna enjoy every minute of it!"

Chapter 14

Longarm made a grab for the gun at his feet, but before he could reach it the whip slashed viciously across his chest, leaving behind a red stripe that oozed blood. He staggered back a step from the force of the whip landing and the pain it brought with it.

Hennigan advanced toward him, arm blurring as he popped the whip again and again. Longarm had to retreat and lift his arms to protect his eyes. He knew that if the leaded tip struck one of them, the eye would be turned to jelly.

That meant he took slash after agonizing slash across his arms, though. He had to find a way to deflect Hennigan's attack, or the overseer might make good on the threat to flay the skin off him.

Longarm's leg bumped against one of the wicker armchairs. He reached down and grabbed it and flung it at Hennigan. The overseer stumbled as the chair hit his legs. He cursed, righted himself, and kicked the chair aside.

That brief respite gave Longarm the chance to vault onto the bed and somersault over it to the other side, where he had left his clothing on the other armchair when he undressed. The deadly little .41-caliber derringer was in his vest pocket, waiting for him to get his hands on it and use it against Hennigan.

The whip struck him on his left shoulder and laid a line of fire across his skin as he reached for the derringer. At the same time the tip swung in front of his throat and circled around it, coiling in a loop like a lariat being dabbed around a steer's neck by a skilled cowboy. Hennigan jerked the loop tight and hauled back on the whip with all the strength in his burly frame.

Longarm felt his air cut off and the choking pain of the whip wrapped around his neck. He fell backward on his haunches. Hennigan rushed up behind him and grabbed the whip, twisting it to tighten the loop around Longarm's neck. He leaned over the big lawman and said harshly, "How do you like bein' strangled, you bastard? Maybe I'll just choke the life out of you!"

Longarm knew Hennigan wasn't far from accomplishing that goal. He reached up and back, locked his hands together behind Hennigan's head, and pulled the overseer down as he lifted himself up. The top of his head crashed into Hennigan's face. Hennigan grunted in pain, and some of the pressure on Longarm's neck went away. The whip was still looped around it, though, and represented a deadly threat.

Longarm drove an elbow backward, striking blindly but hoping the blow would land on Hennigan's crotch. He got the overseer's thigh instead, but the impact was enough to knock Hennigan back a step anyway. Longarm clawed at the whip, got his fingers under it, and tore it away. His throat burned, and even though he couldn't see it, he knew there was a bad abrasion all around it.

He couldn't worry about such things now. Instead he twisted and tackled Hennigan around the waist. The overseer was already off balance, so as Longarm drove hard with his legs, he was able to force Hennigan off his feet

144

and send the overseer crashing heavily to the floor on his back.

Longarm scrambled on top of the man and used his left hand to grab Hennigan's right wrist. He pinned it to the floor, bunched his right hand into a fist, and smashed it a couple of times into Hennigan's face. The hand throbbed from the gash on the back of it, but Longarm didn't care. He was able to ignore the pain as long as he was handing some out to Hennigan.

The overseer was half stunned, and blood welled from his lips where Longarm had smashed them. But he was still able to sledge his mallet-like left fist into the side of Longarm's head. The lawman rolled against the wall as the force of Hennigan's blow knocked him off.

Longarm kicked Hennigan in the chest. He couldn't let the man bring that whip into play again. In Hennigan's hands it was as deadly as a knife or a tomahawk or any other close-range weapon. Longarm leaped to his feet and made another grab for the derringer, but Hennigan hooked a booted foot around his ankles and jerked them out from under him.

Longarm fell again, this time across the bed where he had recently enjoyed such fantastic lovemaking with Cecilia.

Too bad it had been followed by betrayal.

He rolled over, the soft mattress seeming to fight him and hold him down. He grabbed the comforter that had been kicked to the foot of the bed while he and Cecilia were cavorting and flung it over Hennigan's head, momentarily blinding him. Hennigan roared with rage as he tried to struggle free of the comforter. He couldn't use the whip, either, while he was enveloped in the bedding.

Longarm leaped at him, slugging with both fists. The blows crashed against Hennigan's head and body, driving him back against the wall. Hennigan sagged, and Longarm knew the overseer was only half conscious now. He put his hands on the top of Hennigan's head and forced it down as he brought his knee up. The knee exploded against Hennigan's face. The comforter absorbed some of the force of the blow, but not enough to keep Hennigan from being knocked senseless. He collapsed on the floor, blood already soaking through the comforter from the nose that had been pulped by Longarm's knee.

Longarm knew he wasn't out of the woods yet. He had disposed of one threat, at least for the moment, but Coffin Hill was full of others. He started to swing around toward the doorway . . .

That was when something slammed into the side of his head with such force that it seemed the whole world had blown up right before his eyes. He felt himself falling, and as he did he caught a glimpse of Cecilia Blanchard standing there, still naked, clutching the gun he had dropped earlier. She held it by the barrel, and even as his consciousness faded he knew that she had swung the butt of the gun against his head with all the strength in her small but well-muscled body.

"You should have done like I wanted, Custis," he heard her say. Her voice was so tiny it sounded like she was a hundred miles away. "But you're not worth shit to me now."

That was the last thing he knew for what seemed like a very long time.

When he clawed and fought his way back to consciousness, the first thing he was aware of was the smell. A fetid stench filled his nostrils. Had Hennigan thrown him into the swamp, as Cecilia said the overseer did with men he wanted to dispose of, or just dumped him into an outhouse?

Neither one, he guessed as something cool and soft touched his face. It felt like a damp cloth, and as it was wiped over his battered features, it brought some relief to the devilish throbbing that filled his skull.

146

"He's alive," said a man's voice. "Looks like he's coming around, too."

Longarm forced his eyes open. That effort drained him of what little strength he had. He lay there unable to move and watched the room spin crazily around him. That included the bearded face of the man who hovered over him. Longarm's muscles convulsed, rolling him onto his side. His head hung off the low bunk or whatever it was he was lying on, and his stomach spasmed. He emptied the contents of his belly with no thought of where it was going.

"Oh, well," said the same voice that had spoken earlier, "at least it's not going to make the place smell any worse than it already does."

Longarm flopped onto his back again. His face was covered with greasy drops of sweat. He lay there with his chest rising and falling raggedly.

Within a few minutes he started to feel stronger. The room settled down and stopped spinning, and he got his first good look at it—and at the man who hunkered beside the bunk.

The walls were made of unpainted, weather-warped planks. There was no ceiling; the rafters were bare and Longarm could see the underside of an equally dilapidated roof. The floor was dirt and had puddles of standing water on it that had seeped up from the soggy ground and dripped in during rainstorms. The room was fairly large and the walls were lined with low, crude bunks. The thin straw mattresses on those bunks were infested with bugs. Longarm felt them crawling on him.

The stink in the room came from piles and puddles of human waste. Who would piss and shit in the same room where they slept?

Folks who didn't have any choice, supposed Longarm. The shack had only one door and no windows, and he would have been willing to bet the door was locked.

He would have wagered, too, that he was inside the old slave quarters.

The place was lit by a single flickering candle stuck on a rough shelf. In the glow from that candle, Longarm studied the haggard face of the man who knelt beside him. The hombre seemed to be fairly young, although his face was lined with strain and exhaustion and there were touches of gray in his shaggy dark hair and matted beard. Something about him seemed familiar, and when Longarm imagined that the features weren't quite so gaunt, he knew what it was.

"You're Matthew Chadwick," he said, his voice coming out of his sore throat as a strangled croak.

The man's blue eyes widened in surprise. "How did you know that?"

"Gimme a hand . . . sitting up. I'll tell you . . . all about it."

Chadwick helped Longarm into a sitting position on the edge of the bunk. Moving made Longarm's head spin again, but it settled down after a moment. A naturally rugged constitution and a very active life had given him the ability to bounce back quickly.

He looked around the room and saw that there were maybe a dozen other men crowded in here. Most of them were varying shades of black, but there were a couple of white men besides him and Matthew Chadwick.

"Did my father send you to look for me?" asked Chadwick. "When Hennigan and a couple of those other bastards brought you in here and dumped you, we figured you were just some poor son of a bitch they'd caught and roughed up, like the rest of us."

"I'm a deputy U.S. marshal," said Longarm. "Name of Custis Long. I was sent down here to find you . . . or find out what happened to you. All your pa or anybody else knew was that you'd disappeared."

"I was kidnapped," Chadwick said grimly. "Led into a trap by—"

"Pierre Jacquard."

Chadwick nodded. "That's right. What else do you know, Marshal?"

"That Tristam Blanchard is a madman and Sheriff Duquesne down in Saint Angelique is working with him. Did Duquesne know about you being grabbed?"

"Not that I'm aware of," replied Chadwick with a shrug. "I didn't even speak to the man while I was in Saint Angelique. He may not have known I was there."

"I don't think he did, but when I showed up to look for you, he figured out quick enough what must have happened to you. That's why he killed Jacquard before I could talk to him."

Chadwick's eyebrows rose. "Jacquard is dead?"

"Yep."

"Good. I hope he burns in hell and keeps the place plenty hot for Blanchard and Hennigan and the others."

One of the other men said despairingly, "Best not talk like that, Matt. The overseers might have spies in here."

"I don't care," snapped Chadwick. "It's the truth."

Without mentioning where he had gotten the information, Longarm quickly detailed what he knew about the evil scheme being carried out by Blanchard, Hennigan, and Duquesne. Chadwick and the others nodded in confirmation. Several of the men in the cabin were from Pont-a-Mousson and had been kidnapped from there.

"How many prisoners are being held here?" asked Longarm.

"There are two more shacks like this one full of men, and one of women," said Chadwick. "So, somewhere between forty and fifty altogether, I'd say."

Longarm shook his head. "Why? Just to recreate a time that's over and done with? Blanchard could have hired workers if he wanted to. He's got the money to pay Hennigan and the other overseers and keep Duquesne working for him."

"You said it yourself, Marshal. He's a madman."

Chadwick was right. Blanchard had to be insane. Hennigan, Duquesne, and the others worked for him because a crazy man's money spent just as well as anybody else's.

"There's something you don't know, Chadwick," Longarm said slowly. "Blanchard has your cousin Natalie. I ran into her in Saint Angelique. She came down here to look for you, too."

A look of horror washed over Chadwick's face. "Natalie?" he said in a husky half whisper. "In the hands of that lunatic?"

"I'm afraid so. Hennigan grabbed her last night while we were staying with Andres Boulware at Pont-a-Mousson."

"You brought Natalie out here into this hellish wilderness?" Chadwick's voice rose in anger. "How could you do that, Marshal?"

"She threatened to come on her own if I didn't bring her," Longarm explained. "She said she'd be better off with me, where I could keep an eye on her, than wandering around on her own." A bitter grimace crossed his face. "I thought she was right about that, but maybe not. Things couldn't have turned out much worse, I reckon."

Chadwick sat down on the bunk beside Longarm and hung his head in his hands. "Natalie," he murmured. "I can't believe it. I just can't believe it. Do you know if she's all right? Have they hurt her?"

"I haven't seen her, but they don't have any reason to hurt her. Fact of the matter is, with her uncle being a U.S. senator and all, they'll probably try to keep her safe, at least for the time being."

"But they can't ever let her go," said Chadwick with an edge of hysteria creeping into his voice. "Or you, or me. If we ever got away from here, we could ruin everything for Blanchard."

Longarm knew what the young man meant. If any of the other prisoners escaped and carried word to the outside world of what was going on here, they might not be believed. Blanchard might be able to bluff his way through any trouble. But a federal lawman and the son and niece of a senator were different stories. Their word would carry more weight. There would be an investigation, and Blanchard's brutal, murderous attempt to cling to the past would be doomed.

Eventually, Blanchard was bound to figure out that the smartest thing for him to do would be to have Longarm, Natalie, and Chadwick shot in the head and dumped in the swamp.

"That means our time is limited and we don't have anything to lose," said Longarm.

"But what can we do?" Chadwick asked.

"Figure out some way to get out of here." Longarm's face was set in grim lines as he added, "And then we'll bring Blanchard's little house of cards crashing right down around him."

There would be no escape on this night. Longarm wasn't in good enough shape for that. He needed some time to rest and think. He spent most of the night picking Chadwick's brain, even after the other men had gone to sleep, claimed by the exhaustion that resulted from their long hours of work in the plantation's fields.

"Has anybody ever tried to dig out of one of these shacks?" he asked.

"You can't dig in this gumbo," replied Chadwick with a shake of his head. "That's the first thing I thought of, too, and I even tried it. Any hole you dig either collapses or fills up with water almost before you start."

"What about busting down the door?"

"It's reinforced with extra beams around it, and there's a heavy padlock."

Longarm scratched at his jaw. "Bust out through the walls themselves, then. This place looks like a strong wind would blow it down."

"It's sturdier than it looks." Chadwick shrugged. "But that's a possibility. At least it would be if we weren't all too tired to do anything like that by the time we've been worked in the fields for fourteen hours a day. Just about everyone is half sick all the time, too, from the bad food and the dampness."

Longarm nodded. Several of the men had lingering coughs. Others had violently loose bowels. It was hard to raise an army in a hellhole like this. That was one more reason to act quickly, before his own condition became too run-down.

"Do you know how many men Blanchard has working for him?" he asked Chadwick.

"Overseers and guards, you mean? About a dozen, I'd say."

That jibed with what Cecilia had told Longarm.

"Doesn't seem like many men to guard fifty prisoners," he said.

Chadwick laughed humorlessly. "It's plenty when we're kept in as bad a shape as we are. Besides, any time we're out of our quarters, we're under the guns of several riflemen. Any of us get out of line and we're dead, just like that."

"And Blanchard and Hennigan make sure you know that," muttered Longarm.

"It's not a bluff, if that's what you're thinking. I haven't been here even a full month, and I've already seen two men shot down for trying to run. I hate to say it's hopeless, Marshal, but I don't see what we can do."

Longarm didn't want Chadwick to get too discouraged, so he changed the subject by asking, "Do you know anything about a fella with a bad limp?"

"You mean the limping man? I've heard talk about him, but I've never seen him myself. The people who live in these parts seem to be afraid of him, if he really exists."

"He exists, all right," said Longarm. "I've seen him a

couple of times with my own eyes. I thought at first he must have some connection with Blanchard, but it doesn't seem like that's the case."

Chadwick shook his head. "If there's any connection, I'm not aware of it. Of course, I don't really know what's been going on since I got tossed in this cesspool."

They were silent for a few minutes. Since all the other men were asleep, Longarm asked quietly, "What about that treasure you came looking for?"

"You know about that, too?"

Longarm nodded. "I don't guess you had a chance to search for it before Jacquard led you into that trap."

"On the contrary," said Chadwick. "I found it."

Longarm looked over at him in surprise.

"In my research, I found an old diary written by one of Jean Lafitte's men," Chadwick went on. "It was in the library of a church in New Orleans. The pirate had gotten religion and left all his worldly goods to the church when he died. A watertight chest containing the treasure is buried under a mangrove tree in the swamp two miles due north of here."

"Then you *didn't* actually find it," said Longarm.

"Well, I haven't dug it up and put my hands on it yet," Chadwick said. "But I know where it is. I won't have any trouble finding it if I ever get out of here . . . which is pretty doubtful."

"I've found it's always best to eat the apple one bite at a time. I don't aim to let Blanchard get away with this if there's anything I can do about it."

Chadwick sighed but didn't say anything. He didn't have to. It was clear he thought they were all doomed.

Eventually Chadwick dozed off, and so did Longarm. It seemed like he had just closed his eyes when the rattle of the padlock on the door roused him.

Then the door was slammed open, a bullwhip cracked, and Hank Hennigan's harsh voice bellowed, "On your feet, you lazy bastards! You got a full day's work to do!"

Chapter 15

Longarm pulled himself up off the mattress, scratching at the bites left on him by the bunk's other inhabitants. The gash on the back of his hand was crusted over with dried blood, as were the other cuts inflicted on him by Hennigan's whip the night before. He was incredibly thirsty, and his stomach was empty.

"Don't we get anything to eat?" he growled at Hennigan as the prisoners shuffled outside into the green shaded light of early morning.

"You'll eat in the fields, after you've put in some work to deserve it." Hennigan had coiled the bullwhip, but he lashed the coil against Longarm's bare back, staggering him. "Now move!"

"Don't I even get my clothes?"

A man Longarm hadn't seen before stood outside with Hennigan. He had a rifle tucked under his arm and a bundle of some sort in his hands. He tossed it to Longarm and said, "There you go, mister. Don't expect us to be so kind to you all the time, though."

Longarm saw that the bundle consisted of his shirt and trousers, which were wrapped around his boots. Clumsily, he pulled them on as he continued to walk along the trail with the other prisoners, prodded by Hennigan and the other guard. It felt good to be dressed again, even though his situation was still pretty damned dire.

About thirty men were assembled for the day's work. Not everyone from all the shacks turned out. Some men were too sick to labor in the fields, and others had chores around the plantation house. With the guards following them on horseback, the "slaves" were marched out to the field where Longarm had seen them working the day before.

When they got there, he saw that a wagon was parked nearby with three more overseers on it. The men handed out hoes to the prisoners, and they were put to work cleaning out weeds and rocks from the field, which obviously hadn't been cultivated in a while.

It was hard work—not as hard as busting rocks on a chain gang, maybe, but still plenty backbreaking, especially for men who weren't in good physical condition to start with. True to what Hennigan had said, the prisoners were forced to labor for a couple of hours before a break was called. Then they were each given a hunk of stale bread and some greasy salt pork, which they washed down with dippers of tepid water from an open barrel in the back of the wagon. Longarm saw things wiggling in the water. No wonder most of the men were sick all the time. The actual slaves who had toiled here at Coffin Hill before the war had been taken better care of than this.

Despite everything, Longarm's brain was still working. Without being too obvious about it, he searched for the hidden riflemen whose godlike power of life and death over these prisoners kept the poor wretches from daring to attempt an escape. He spotted reflections off metal at several places in the trees around the field and knew that was the sun glinting off rifle barrels.

If he could get his own hands on a rifle, he figured he stood a good chance of killing or wounding at least a couple of the hidden riflemen before they could start firing. But that was a mighty big "if."

In the middle of the day, as the sun was beating down mercilessly in this cleared field, the men were allowed to stop again for a short time. This time they got only a piece of bread and a dipper of water. When the break was over, the wagon drove off toward the plantation house, leaving only Hennigan and the other guard to watch over the workers, plus the riflemen in the trees.

Longarm wondered what would happen if he jumped one of the guards. Would the other men try to help him and seize the chance to escape? He sensed Chadwick would; the young man hadn't been a prisoner for so long that his spirit and will to live were broken.

The others, though, seemed gripped by despair as well as by illness and exhaustion. A few might try to help him, but he couldn't count on much assistance from any of them.

The men were scattered out. Longarm began working his way unobtrusively toward Matthew Chadwick, hoping for a chance to alert the young man that he was going to try a break. Before he got there, though, a yell suddenly burst out from one of the other men.

"Look up yonder! Fire!"

Longarm jerked around and gazed where the man was pointing. A column of thick black smoke poured up into the sky. With the trees screening the field it was hard to tell exactly where the smoke was coming from, but it looked to Longarm like the plantation house itself or one of the outbuildings was burning.

"Damn it!" yelled Hennigan. He wheeled his horse and shouted to the other guard, "Get 'em back up to the house as fast as you can! We may need 'em to fight that fire!"

Then he banged his heels into his horse's flanks and sent the animal galloping toward the house.

Longarm knew a stroke of luck when he saw it. Brandishing a rifle, the other guard began rounding up the workers. Most of them stumbled along compliantly, afraid of the hidden riflemen. Longarm pretended to do so himself, until the man came within reach. Then Longarm struck with the hoe he still carried, slashing upward at the man in the saddle.

The guard saw the attack coming and twisted in the saddle as he tried to bring his rifle to bear on Longarm. The weapon's barrel clashed with the hoe handle. That prevented the hoe from striking the guard, but it also knocked the rifle out of his hand. Longarm dropped the hoe and leaped upward, grabbing the guard and pulling him out of the saddle.

He hoped that as long as he was so close to this guard, the riflemen would hold their fire for fear of hitting their comrade. As a bullet whined past his ear, he realized that wasn't the case. He slammed his right fist into the guard's belly and doubled the man over. At the same time, he used his left hand to pluck the revolver from the holster on the guard's hip. He crashed the gun into the side of the guard's head and laid him out cold.

Another slug sizzled through the air next to Longarm's ear. He dived for the rifle the guard had dropped, came up with it, and caught the dangling reins of the man's horse. Turning the animal so that its body partially shielded him from the rifle fire, he rested the rifle on the saddle and drew a bead on the woods where powder smoke drifted up. Longarm cranked off a couple of rounds as quickly as he could work the rifle's lever, then sprayed more lead toward the positions where he had spotted the riflemen earlier.

"Run!" he shouted to the other men during a lull in the shooting. "Spread out and run, damn it! They can't get all of you!"

The men had been milling around aimlessly, apparently confused about what was going on, but now several of them broke into shambling runs toward the nearest trees. More followed, until the whole group had broken into a stampede. A couple of men fell, knocked off their feet by rifle fire, but the others reached the safety of the trees.

All except for Matthew Chadwick, who dashed over to Longarm and said, "We have to get to Natalie!"

Longarm had been thinking the same thing. He snapped another shot at the hidden gunmen as he said, "Get on this horse!"

Chadwick took the reins and vaulted into the saddle. He leaned forward to make a smaller target of himself as he extended a hand to Longarm. The big lawman grasped it and swung up behind Chadwick, who then kicked the horse into a run. Longarm clung to the animal's back with his knees as he continued firing the rifle toward the enemy.

Riding double, the two men galloped out of the field. Longarm hoped everybody at the plantation house was too occupied with the fire to have noticed the shooting in the field. At the very least, quite a few of the "slaves" had gotten away. Maybe some of them would be able to bring help back here.

They came in sight of the house and saw that it wasn't ablaze. The barn was burning fiercely, though, and so were several outbuildings. Longarm felt a surge of relief. He figured Natalie was being held prisoner somewhere in the house. The idea that she might have been trapped in there while it burned had worried him.

As Chadwick brought the horse to a halt in front of Coffin Hill, Longarm pulled out the six-gun he had tucked in the waistband of his trousers and pressed it into the young man's hands. "You know how to use a revolver?"

"Well enough," said Chadwick.

"I'll hang on to the rifle, then. Come on. It looked like everybody was out back fighting that fire, so maybe we can find Natalie before they realize what's going on."

They hurried into the house. Longarm wasn't fond of

the idea of splitting up, but they could cover more ground in their search that way.

"Take this floor," he said to Chadwick. "I'll check upstairs."

He bounded up the grand, curving staircase, taking the steps three at a time. When he reached the main hallway on the second floor, he called, "Natalie! Natalie, are you up here?"

He threw open doors as he passed them, but the rooms were all empty. Suddenly, the sound of a muffled scream came to his ears from behind one of the doors he hadn't reached yet. He raised his foot and crashed it against the panel beside the knob. With a splintering of wood, the door was torn open and slammed back against the wall inside the room.

Longarm froze as he saw not only Natalie but Cecilia Blanchard. Cecilia stood behind the older girl with an arm looped around Natalie's neck and the sharp point of a knife at her throat.

"Custis, what's going on?" she demanded. "It . . . it sounds like everything has gone insane outside."

"A lot of the slaves have already escaped," Longarm told her. "The barn's on fire, and so are some of the other buildings." He decided to take a chance. "If you really want to get out of here like you said, drop that knife and come with Natalie and me."

"Take me, but she stays here," said Cecilia.

Longarm shook his head. "That ain't the way it's got to be."

Cecilia's nostrils flared. "It will be if this bitch is dead!"

Longarm snapped the rifle to his shoulder, ready to try a risky shot even though Cecilia was mostly concealed behind Natalie. It was a slim chance but maybe the only one Natalie had.

But before he could press the trigger, Natalie twisted desperately in Cecilia's grip. The tip of the blade cut the side of Natalie's neck and drew a yelp of pain from her, but that didn't stop her from sinking an elbow into Cecilia's midsection. That knocked Cecilia back a step, so that Natalie was able to pivot and slam a punch into her jaw. The blow sent Cecilia sprawling onto the bed. She dropped the knife.

Longarm stepped forward quickly and kicked the blade under the bed, out of easy reach. He caught hold of Natalie's arm and asked, "Are you all right?"

"Now that you're here I am, Custis," she said. Blood trickled from the cut on her neck, but it didn't look serious.

Longarm cast a last glance at the stunned Cecilia, then said, "Let's get out of here," and tugged Natalie toward the door. They ran out, leaving the younger woman there. Longarm felt a little sorry for Cecilia, because he knew she wanted to get away from her lunatic father, but he didn't trust her. She would be able to get out from under Blanchard's thumb soon enough, once the crazed plantation owner was behind bars where he belonged.

As they clattered down the stairs, Longarm shouted, "Chadwick! I've got her!"

Natalie gasped. "Matthew's alive?"

"Yeah, and with me. We just broke loose together."

As they reached the bottom of the staircase, Chadwick came running from the direction of the dining room. "Natalie!" he cried.

They grabbed each other and hugged tightly. Longarm let the reunion between the cousins go on for a moment, then said, "We'd better get out of here while we've got the chance."

Chadwick nodded and took Natalie's hand. "Come on."

As they ran out the front door of the house, Longarm saw that the horse was still there where they had left it. He was grateful for that.

But he didn't get much time to experience that gratitude, because at that moment several men came running around the corner of the house, including Tristam Blanchard and Hank Hennigan. "Stop them!" Blanchard shouted stridently.

Longarm flung the rifle to his shoulder and fired a couple of rounds. The bullets came close enough to make Blanchard, Hennigan, and the other men duck back around the corner. Hennigan hurriedly fired a pistol at them as he retreated. The slugs missed Longarm and his companions by a large margin, but one of them burned across the rump of the horse. The animal let out a shrill whinny of pain and bolted away in a dead run.

Longarm bit back a curse. He knew that all three of them couldn't have ridden on the horse anyway, not and make it very far, but he had hoped that Chadwick and Natalie could get away on the animal. Now that chance was gone.

"Head for the swamp!" he told them as he continued to lay down covering fire. He didn't like the idea of fleeing into that dismal wasteland, but out on the trail they would have no chance of getting away. Hennigan and the remaining guards would run them down in no time on horseback. At least in the swamp they might be able to give their pursuers the slip.

Longarm ran after the cousins, twisting to snap more shots at the plantation house. Bullets continued to whine around him, and one even came close enough to tug at his sleeve. His luck couldn't last forever.

Luckily, the swamp came up close to Coffin Hill in places, and a moment later Longarm plunged into the thick vegetation and shallow, murky water. Spanish moss brushed his face. He paused just inside the swamp to turn and fire a couple of final shots at the house, hoping to slow down the pursuit, but the rifle's hammer clicked harmlessly when he pulled the trigger. The weapon was empty.

He threw it aside, not wanting it to slow him down. He ran, water splashing high around his legs as he fled. He slipped and fell a couple of times, drenching himself and coating his clothes with mud.

That was the beginning of a desperate flight through the swamp. Longarm had no idea which direction he was going, and in the watery green light that seemed to come from everywhere and nowhere at the same time, there was no way for him to orient himself. He didn't know where Chadwick and Natalie were, only that they were ahead of him somewhere. He didn't try to be quiet. Instead he made as much noise as he could, hoping that he would draw the pursuit away from the others.

Time passed, though Longarm couldn't have said how much. It seemed to have no meaning in this watery wasteland. Every now and then he heard the baying of hounds behind him, along with an occasional shout. He hadn't seen any bloodhounds at Coffin Hill, but it didn't surprise him that Blanchard had some of the beasts. Every crazy plantation owner stuck in the past needed hounds to track down runaway slaves, didn't he?

Battered and bruised and cut from the fight with Hennigan the night before, weary from lack of sleep, sore and exhausted from the morning's work in the field, Longarm felt his strength deserting him. He had more reserves than most men, but even his body had limits beyond which he could not push it. He sensed that he was getting close to those limits now. But since he hadn't caught up with Chadwick and Natalie, he hoped that they had taken some other route and would be safe once they emerged from the swamp. It might take them some time to reach civilization, but once they did, they would be able to summon help.

One way or another, Blanchard's empire was going to crumble.

The men and the hounds were closing in. Longarm went to ground on a grassy hummock, hoping the pursuers would go past without seeing him in the tall growth. They were practically on top of him. . . .

That was when the damn gator came up behind him and waddled toward him, ready to grab him by the leg and drag him underwater to its den, where his body would rot and form a nice feast for the scaly monster.

Longarm couldn't hold back the shout of horror that welled up in his throat as the alligator lunged at him. He rolled aside desperately.

"There he is!" yelled one of the men. "Let the dogs loose!"

Baying madly, the hounds rushed onto the hummock, but they stopped short when they saw the gator. The massive reptile was confused and turned away from Longarm toward the dogs. The two men charged onto the higher ground right behind the hounds. They almost tripped over the dogs, who were backing up now and growling furiously as the gator came toward them.

"Shit!" one of the men cried. "It's a gator!"

They opened up with their rifles, pouring lead into the swamp creature as fast as they could work the levers and pull the triggers. The blasts filled the air like thunder and sent colorful birds flying in alarm from the low-hanging branches of the trees.

The slugs smashed into the gator but didn't stop it right away. The creature waddled on, absorbing the lead thrown at it. Inevitably, though, death caught up to it and its short legs folded up underneath it. The alligator collapsed as blood gushed from its numerous wounds.

That left Longarm at the mercy of the men who had been chasing him. He scrambled to his feet as the hounds came at him. "Get away!" he snarled as he kicked at the dogs.

One of the men grabbed the dogs and pulled them back while the other one covered Longarm. Both of them grinned. Longarm hadn't seen them before, but they were cut from the same brutal cloth as Hank Hennigan. He could

164

tell that by looking at their coarse, beard-stubbled faces and rawboned bodies.

"I knew we'd catch up to you sooner or later, boy," drawled the man holding his rifle on Longarm. "Ain't nobody knows this swamp better'n us."

A new voice said, "There's one."

Both men cursed and started to swing around toward the figure that had loomed up suddenly behind them. They were too late. The man held an old-fashioned flintlock pistol in each fist. He thrust the guns out in front of him and fired. Black powder roared and smoke billowed as the heavy lead balls slammed into the chests of the two men from Coffin Hill. They were driven back off their feet by the impact. The one holding the hounds' leashes let go of them. The dogs ran away, whining as if they were terrified.

As well they might have been. As the stranger lowered his guns and the cloud of powder smoke drifted away, Longarm saw the long coat and the slouch hat. Under the drooping brim was a face so gaunt it resembled a skull. A black patch covered the left eye, while the right regarded Longarm with a look of piercing fire. Lank gray hair fell to bony shoulders. The man looked like walking death.

Limping death, actually, as he started toward Longarm, heavily favoring his right leg as he climbed onto the hummock.

Chapter 16

Longarm knew those pistols were single-shot weapons, so until they were reloaded they wouldn't do the limping man any good unless he intended to club somebody to death with them. Longarm didn't figure to let that happen.

"Hold on there, old son," he said tightly. "It ain't that I'm not obliged to you for blasting those two to perdition, but who are you and what do you want with me?"

"Only to save your life, M'sieu Long," said the stranger in a harsh rasp of a voice, "and to reunite you with your two friends."

Longarm frowned. "My friends?"

He heard splashing and turned his head to see Natalie and Chadwick wading through the swamp toward him. "Custis!" cried Natalie. "You're all right!"

"Yeah," said Longarm with a nod. "Thanks to this fella here."

The limping man tucked the empty pistols behind a wide belt that encircled his waist under the long coat. "Lucien Farnol, at your service, Marshal," he introduced himself.

"You know who I am?"

"I know who all of you are. Nothing happens in the swamps of Terrenoire Parish without me knowing about it.

They have been my home for many years, since the days I sailed with Jean Lafitte himself."

Longarm's brain was whirling. All this was going too fast for him to keep up. The limping man, that sinister figure who had the whole countryside terrified, had just saved his life and had obviously led Natalie and Chadwick here, too. And now he claimed to have been one of Lafitte's pirates. . . . ?

Farnol's thin lips curved slightly, and Longarm realized that counted as a smile on the skull-like face. "I see you are confused," said Farnol. "I will explain everything . . . but not here." He held up a hand, signaling for them to listen. In the distance sounded the baying of more hounds. "Come with me," added Farnol, gesturing curtly for them to follow him. "The pursuers will follow the sound of those shots."

He led the way through the swamp, seeming to have an unerring instinct for the best paths to follow and the dangers to avoid. Longarm was right behind him, then Natalie, with Chadwick bringing up the rear.

As Farnol stalked along, he turned his head and said over his shoulder, "I was outside the slave quarters last night and overheard you explaining everything to our young friend here through a gap in the wall. Even before that, though, I suspected you were a lawman M'sieu Long, because of the way you kept turning up everywhere there was trouble."

Longarm grunted. "The same thing could be said of you, old son."

Farnol chuckled hollowly. "I know my reputation in these parts as some sort of spectral being. I have done nothing to discourage it. I did not want anyone coming into the swamps to disrupt my search."

"Search for what?" asked Longarm, although he had a hunch he already knew the answer.

"Captain Lafitte's treasure."

"The treasure!" exclaimed Chadwick. "But I know right where it is!"

Farnol stopped and swung around sharply. "*Mon dieu!* You know where the treasure is hidden?"

Chadwick nodded. "I found the location in the diary of Anton Lafleur."

"The Flower?" Farnol leaned over and spat into the water. "He knew nothing!"

Chadwick's eyes widened in disbelief. "But . . . but his diary . . . I found it in a church in New Orleans. . . . He wrote the exact location of the treasure in it."

Farnol tapped a finger against his temple. "A musket ball struck Lafleur here during the battle as we were boarding a British merchantman one time in the gulf. He lived, but after that he was never the same. He lived in a world of his own and made up stories all day. Lafitte took pity on him and allowed him to live at Barataria, but nothing he said . . . or wrote down . . . could be believed."

Chadwick covered his face with his hands. "All for nothing," he moaned. "It was all for nothing. There's probably not even a treasure—"

"Ah, but no, the treasure exists," said Farnol. "Of that I am sure."

"If you were one of Lafitte's men," said Longarm, "how come you don't know where the loot's cached?"

"Because the captain took only a handful of men with him, his brother-in-law Dominique You and a few others, when he hid the treasure. I was a very young man, relatively new to Lafitte's crew, and was not included in the party. None of them ever revealed the hiding place. They are all dead now, but the treasure is still out here somewhere."

"And you've been looking for it."

Farnol nodded. "As I said, the search has consumed years of my life."

"You know what Blanchard's been up to on his plantation?"

"I know," Farnol said grimly. "I have seen his men waylay unwary travelers and take men and women by force from the settlement started by the man they call Bullroar."

"And you just let him get away with it?" Longarm couldn't keep the anger out of his voice.

"It was not my job to stop him."

"No, your job is to hunt for some damn pirate treasure!"

Natalie touched Longarm's sleeve. "Custis, he *did* help us. He found Matthew and me and brought us right to you. And he saved you from Blanchard's men."

"I know it," Longarm admitted in a grudging tone. "But he could have tried to do something about Blanchard a long time ago."

"Perhaps the authorities should have investigated Blanchard a long time ago," said Farnol. "At any rate, I stepped in and took a hand as soon as I could once an actual lawman arrived here. Who do you think started those fires at Coffin Hill so you would have a chance to escape?"

Longarm stared at him for a second and then shrugged. Natalie was right; Farnol *had* helped them, and the old pirate seemed to want to do the right thing now. Better late than never, he supposed.

"Come along," said Farnol. "The hounds are getting closer, and we do not want Hennigan and the others to catch up to us . . . until we are ready for them."

"What do you mean by that?"

"Blanchard will not let his men rest until they have run you to ground. Your only chance is to make sure that when they catch you, it is in a place of your own choosing. A place of *my* choosing, I should say, where we can deal with them."

Longarm nodded, knowing that what Farnol said made sense. "All right, lead the way."

The little group plunged deeper and deeper into the swamp, until they came to a clearing about twenty feet wide and forty feet across. Farnol threw out an arm to stop the others.

"We must go around," he said. "Carefully now. Step only where I step."

"What's out there?" asked Longarm as his eyes narrowed in suspicion.

"Quicksand," replied Farnol. "Very dangerous."

Longarm looked at the clearing. The grass was a bit more sparse than normal, but the ground that was visible appeared solid enough. Those appearances could be deceptive, though.

Slowly and cautiously, the four of them made their way around the clearing to a stand of mangrove trees on the far side that bordered a stretch of open water. Longarm, Natalie, and Chadwick were careful to step only where Farnol placed his feet. Longarm breathed a small sigh of relief when they were past the quicksand. However, his forehead creased in a frown when he looked around and realized how narrow the strip of solid ground was where the mangroves grew. They would need a boat of some sort to cross the water, or else they would be trapped here with no place to go.

The hunters and the hounds were closing in rapidly. The baying was loud now, and the shouts of the men with the dogs were clearly audible.

"Now we wait," said Farnol, and Longarm realized that the old pirate intended for the pursuit to end here. This had been Farnol's destination all along.

Farnol took a powderhorn and shot pouch from under his long coat and began reloading his flintlock pistols. "I don't reckon you have another of those blunderbusses, do you, old son?" asked Longarm.

"No. I have carried this brace of pistols for more than sixty years, and they have never failed me." Farnol reached under his coat again and produced a Colt .45 Peacemaker. "But you might be able to make use of this, Marshal. Back at my shack, deep in the swamp, I have quite a collection of weapons I have accumulated over the years."

Longarm grinned as he wrapped his hand around the butt of the Colt. It was the same model he carried and felt mighty good to him right then. He checked the loads and saw that every chamber in the cylinder was filled.

"The odds just got a mite more even," he said.

The four of them spread out, Longarm and Farnol each moving behind one of the mangroves, Natalie and Chadwick taking cover behind a particularly thick trunk. The baying of the hounds grew louder still, and suddenly men and dogs appeared on the far side of the clearing.

"Stop right there!" shouted Farnol, lifting his voice so that all the men could hear him.

The pursuers handling the hounds ducked back sharply into the brush, obviously fearing an ambush. As Longarm peered around the tree trunk, he saw Blanchard and Hennigan among a group carrying rifles. The brush practically bristled with the barrels of the weapons.

"Go back!" Farnol told them. "Leave the swamp! You are not welcome here!"

"Who the hell are you?" bellowed Hennigan.

"Who I am is none of your concern! If you value your lives, turn around and leave, and never come back!"

"Go to hell!" Longarm could hear Hennigan's voice as the overseer went on to Blanchard, "They're hidden over there in those trees. I say we root 'em out!"

Longarm couldn't hear Blanchard's reply, but the pursuers stayed where they were. Maybe Blanchard was wary of losing some of his men in a gun battle. Knowing what he knew, Longarm sort of hated to do what he did next, but Blanchard had to be goaded into action.

"Listen to me, Blanchard!" he called. "You know I'm a federal lawman! I'll be back with the army and you'll spend the rest of your life in prison! And I'll see to it personally that Coffin Hill is burned to the ground!"

That did the trick. Blanchard sputtered for a second in

172

incoherent rage, then screamed, "Get them! Kill them! A thousand dollars to the man who brings me Long's head!"

The men with the dogs charged forward, followed by the riflemen. Hennigan yelled, "Don't kill the girl! She's gonna be mine!"

The hounds made it several yards into the clearing, dragging the men who held their rope leads, before they started to sink. The note of their baying changed from the thrill of the hunt to sheer terror as their canine brains realized that something was wrong. Their handlers began to bog down, too, and hurriedly let go of the leads, but it was too late. They were stuck and sinking. Frantic curses filled the air.

Longarm and Chadwick opened fire with their pistols as the riflemen tried to turn back before the quicksand could claim them. The bullets ripped into the men and drove them off their feet. Some landed on solid ground, but some sprawled on the clinging, deceptively solid-looking muck.

Hennigan was one of the men who escaped. He threw himself clear, rolled over, and came up firing. Longarm dropped to one knee as the bullets from the overseer's rifle chewed splinters from the mangrove trunk a foot above his head. He drew a bead and fired. Hennigan was thrown backward by the slug that drove into his chest. He landed on his back with his arms outflung and writhed in pain for a few seconds before the stillness of death came over him.

"Throw your guns away!" shouted Farnol. "Throw your guns away and we will save all of you we can!"

The terrified men stuck in the quicksand did as they were told, flinging rifles and pistols aside as fast as they could.

"Your comrades, too!" ordered Farnol. "Or no one will be rescued!"

The handful of men still on solid ground hesitated. They looked around as if they expected to receive orders from

Blanchard, but the plantation owner seemed to have fled when he realized that the odds were turning against him. "Where's Blanchard?" one of the men asked. "Where the hell did he go?"

"Better make up your minds in a hurry!" called Longarm. "Otherwise it's gonna be too late for some of you!"

"For God's sake!" screamed one of the men in the quicksand. "Do what they say!"

Instead of surrendering, the men on solid ground suddenly turned and ran, taking off for the tall and uncut rather than staying to face justice. Longarm hated to see any of them get away, but Blanchard was the one he really wanted, and he couldn't go after the plantation owner until things were settled here.

The hounds' instincts had taken over, and instead of struggling against the pull of the quicksand they had tried to swim their way out of it. They were succeeding for the most part, gradually dog-paddling their way clear of the stuff. Longarm was glad to see that.

He and Chadwick stepped out from behind the mangroves and covered the men while Farnol used a big knife he took from under his coat to hack down some thick vines. Using them like ropes, he tossed them to the trapped men and let them pull themselves free of the quicksand. It was a wet, bedraggled, clearly scared bunch that soon huddled under the guns of Longarm and Chadwick and Farnol.

"Can you handle them?" Longarm asked Chadwick and the old pirate. "I want to get back to Coffin Hill and settle up with Blanchard."

Farnol nodded and said, "We can watch them, but can you find your way back to the plantation?"

"I'm damn sure gonna try. Reckon you can point me in the right direction?"

"Keep the water on your left," said Farnol, "and any time you must turn, bear to the right. And always watch where you step."

Longarm glanced at the innocent-appearing quicksand. "I plan to," he said. "Got any more shells for this Colt?"

Farnol took a handful of ammunition from a coat pocket and passed it over to the big lawman. Longarm thumbed fresh cartridges into the revolver and then smiled at Natalie.

"See you back at Coffin Hill," he told her.

"Be careful, Custis," she said. "Watch out for Blanchard . . . and don't trust that girl, either."

"No chance of that," said Longarm.

He hurried off through the swamp, leaving the others to follow at a slower pace with the prisoners. As he followed Farnol's directions, he realized that he was making faster progress than he had in his earlier flight. He must have been running around in circles part of that time, he decided. That would be easy to do in a trackless wasteland like this swamp.

A half hour later he caught a glimpse of the big house through the trees and steered straight toward it. He emerged from the swamp into the overgrown garden at the back of the house.

The barn and the other outbuildings that had been set on fire by Lucien Farnol were now nothing more than heaps of smoking rubble. The flames hadn't spread to the plantation house, though. It was untouched. Longarm moved carefully and silently toward it through the garden. He wondered where Blanchard had gone. The man was probably somewhere inside the house, waiting to see who would come back from the swamp.

Blanchard wasn't going to like the answer to that question.

Longarm reached the rear door of the old mansion. An eerie silence hung over the plantation. All the birds had been frightened away by the shooting. The house seemed deserted. Longarm figured all the servants had fled as soon as they realized this was their chance to get away. They had all been held here against their wills.

He opened the rear door and stepped inside, listening intently. Where would Blanchard hide? The library? His bedroom? Longarm didn't know. He was going to have to search the whole house until he found the man he was after.

The search didn't last long. As he stepped into the big, shadowy dining room he saw movement to his right and whirled in that direction. The Colt in his hand came up, but he didn't fire.

Tristam Blanchard stood there, his hands empty. He held them out toward Longarm and implored, "Don't shoot! For God's sake, please don't shoot!"

A part of Longarm wanted to just blow a hole through the man's evil, rotten brain. But he was a lawman, and he couldn't do that. He said, "You're under arrest, Blanchard."

A floorboard creaked behind Longarm, and it was followed instantly by the metallic sound of a gun being cocked.

"I don't think so," said Sheriff Remy Duquesne.

Chapter 17

"I'd say you're the one who's in a heap of trouble here, Long," continued the crooked lawman. "Here I pay a visit to one of Terrenoire Parish's leading citizens, and I find a crazy man holding a gun on him. Why, it's my duty as sheriff to protect the citizenry and shoot that crazy man."

Longarm glanced over his shoulder and saw Duquesne standing in the double doorway between the dining room and the foyer, holding a leveled revolver. The gun was pointed at Longarm's head.

"It's a mighty good thing I decided to take a ride out here today and make sure everything was all right," Duquesne went on. "Looks to me like all hell's been breaking loose around here."

"Stop yammering and shoot him!" Blanchard cried abruptly. "Shoot him!"

"You know I'm a deputy U.S. marshal," said Longarm. "You can kill me and throw my body to the gators, but my boss will just send somebody else to find out what happened to me."

"Then we'll kill him, too," said Duquesne with a smug smile on his broad, florid face.

"You keep killing deputy marshals, how long do you

think it'll be before the army comes in here to clean up this hellhole?"

Duquesne was still calm. "We'll deal with that when it happens."

"Be smarter to get out while you can."

Duquesne ignored that and ordered, "Drop the gun, Long."

"Why should I do that? You're gonna kill me anyway, aren't you?"

"That's right. But if you cooperate, I'll do it quick. Otherwise I'm liable to just wound you and toss you to the gators while you're still alive. That'd be a bad way to go, I imagine."

Longarm saw movement in the shadows behind the crooked sheriff. From where he stood he could see the staircase leading down to the foyer from the second floor. Someone was coming down those stairs, someone in a long, flowing dress, dark hair tangled around her head, and something in her hands.

"What do you get out of this, Duquesne?" asked Longarm, suddenly aware of how important it was to keep the sheriff talking. "Money? Have you been helping Blanchard all this time just because he pays you? You'd give up your honor, turn your back on the law you swore to uphold, just for some loot?"

Duquesne laughed. "Blanchard pays well. But that ain't all of it. He's promised me that daughter of his, too. Hennigan thinks *he's* getting her, but he doesn't know what's really going on, the dumb bastard. Cecilia Blanchard's going to be mine." Duquesne's glance turned toward the plantation owner for a second. "And I think the time has come for that payoff, Blanchard."

"N-no!" stammered Blanchard. "No!"

And behind Duquesne, Cecilia screamed, "No!" as she pressed both triggers of the shotgun she held in her hands, pointed toward the sheriff's back.

A look of surprise appeared on Duquesne's beefy face as he tried to turn, but he had barely started to move when the roar of the scattergun thundered through the house. The double load of buckshot caught him squarely in the body and blew him apart in a grisly spray of crimson. He was driven off his feet and crashed heavily to the floor. His face was untouched and so were his legs, but his torso was a horrific mass of pulped, shredded, bleeding flesh.

Longarm didn't have time to be sickened by what had happened to Duquesne. A pistol barked behind him and he heard the wind-rip of a bullet past his ear. He spun around and dropped to a knee as he saw that Blanchard had pulled a gun from under his coat.

The plantation owner fired again just as the Colt in Longarm's hand roared and bucked against his palm. Blanchard's second shot went wide, too, but Longarm's bullet caught the plantation owner in the stomach and doubled him over. Blanchard staggered back a couple of steps, caught himself, and tried to raise the pistol in his hand again. Longarm shot him a second time, this round going into Blanchard's chest. It knocked him off his feet. He grabbed the linen tablecloth as he went down and dragged it part of the way off the table as he sprawled on the floor, kicked a couple of times, and died.

Longarm heard a thud. When he turned quickly he saw that Cecilia had dropped the shotgun she had used to kill Duquesne. She looked down at the breast of the gown she wore, where a red flower was blooming. When Longarm saw that, he knew where at least one of Blanchard's stray bullets had gone.

Cecilia said, "Custis . . ." and then crumpled to the gleaming hardwood floor of the foyer.

And Longarm was left there alone, gun in hand, the sharp bite of powder smoke in his nostrils, his heart pounding so hard that the pulse in his head sounded like the rhythm of distant drums.

• • •

"This should be it," said Matthew Chadwick as he rested a hand on the trunk of a giant mangrove tree growing at the edge of a stretch of swamp water.

"I tell you, you cannot place any faith in anything written by Anton Lafleur," insisted Farnol.

Longarm said, "I don't reckon it'll hurt anything to have a look."

Farnol shrugged his bony shoulders. "Do as you wish, but I have come to believe that the treasure of Jean Lafitte will never be found."

"You just don't want it to be found by anyone else," Natalie put in.

Farnol scowled, making his face look more frightening than ever.

Over the past few days, though, Longarm had learned that the old pirate wasn't quite as fearsome as he appeared. Farnol hadn't sailed with Lafitte for very long before deciding that a pirate's life wasn't for him. He had drifted away from that band of rogues and eventually married. His wife had given birth to a daughter who had grown up to be a nun belonging to an order in New Orleans. Farnol's wife had died from a fever not long after the girl was born, and after that Farnol had gone to the swamps to deal with his grief—and to search for Lafitte's treasure. He had admitted to Longarm that if he ever found the loot, he intended to give most of it to the nuns who had raised his daughter and eventually accepted her as one of them.

After the tragic, violent shoot-out at Coffin Hill, Longarm had seen to it that the rest of Blanchard's men were locked up in the jail at Saint Angelique, then he had ridden to the railroad to send a wire to Billy Vail explaining the situation and asking for help. More deputy marshals had been sent from New Orleans, and they would spend the next few weeks cleaning up the mess in Terrenoire Parish. Longarm was supposed to head back to Denver.

But he had this errand to take care of first. He and Chadwick, along with Natalie and Farnol, had ridden out here, picking up Andres Boulware and Davey along the way at Pont-a-Mousson, where there had been many joyous reunions over the last few days. Now all six of them were eager to see what, if anything, Longarm and Chadwick would dig up underneath the mangrove tree.

Farnol kept muttering about how nothing was going to be there, but Longarm and Chadwick continued digging. It wasn't easy because they were soon up to their knees in muddy water and had to use buckets they had brought along to bail out some of the sludge.

"I wonder if this chest Lafitte's supposed to have buried was watertight?" asked Longarm.

"Lafleur's diary said it contained gold, silver, and jewelry, so it wouldn't matter if it was wet," replied Chadwick. "But if he was really mad, like Mr. Farnol says . . ."

The old pirate snorted.

A second later the blade of Longarm's shovel *thunked* against something hard.

"My God!" exclaimed Chadwick. "Did you hear that?"

"I heard it," Longarm said with a grin. "Let's see what we got."

As the others leaned forward eagerly, Longarm and Chadwick continued to dig and use the buckets to clear away the mud and water. With great difficulty, they were finally able to reach down into the muck, grab hold of whatever it was they had found, and wrestle it free of the dark, clinging mud.

They set an old chest about two feet tall, three feet long, and two feet deep on the ground. It was covered with mud, but Natalie was able to use a cloth to clean off the stuff around a hasp that was held closed by a lock.

"Let me see one of those shovels," said Farnol, and despite all the nay-saying he had done, his voice trembled a little with excitement now. He took the shovel and slammed the blade against the lock several times, until the hasp finally tore loose. Farnol tossed the shovel aside.

Carefully, the old pirate lifted the lid.

The greenish sunlight in the swamp gleamed off the gold and silver coins and the jewelry piled inside the chest. "*Mon dieu*," breathed Farnol and Boulware in unison.

"Who does it all belong to?" asked Natalie.

"Mr. Farnol," answered Chadwick without hesitation. "There's a good chance he's the last surviving member of Jean Lafitte's band."

Farnol shook his head. "You should have the lion's share, M'sieu Chadwick. You were the one who believed while I said there was nothing here."

"That doesn't matter—"

"Besides," Farnol went on, "most of it was stolen, so I have no right to it at all. But if you will be so kind as to share your good fortune, I will pass along what you give me to help my daughter and the other nuns feed the poor in New Orleans."

"There's poor folks right here in Terrenoire Parish," Longarm pointed out. "I expect the citizens of Pont-a-Mousson could make good use of some treasure, couldn't they, M'sieu Boulware?"

"Indeed they could," said Boulware.

"It's settled, then," declared Chadwick. "We'll split it up, with shares going to the nuns in New Orleans, the people of Pont-a-Mousson, and Marshal Long, Natalie, and myself."

Longarm shook his head. "Not me. I ain't allowed to keep things like this. I don't get paid forty-a-month-and-found, like I did back in my cowboy days."

"But then you don't get anything out of all this," protested Natalie.

Longarm thought about the people he had helped to free from bondage and torture at the hands of an evil lunatic, and about the justice he had brought to the swampland, and about the moments of pleasure he had shared with the beautiful young woman who was looking at him now.

"I get paid plenty," he said with a smile.

Watch for

LONGARM AND THE DWARF'S DARLING

the 343rd novel in the exciting Longarm series from
Jove

Coming in June!

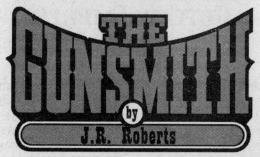

LONGARM

GIANT-SIZED ADVENTURE FROM AVENGING ANGEL LONGARM.

LONGARM AND THE OUTLAW EMPRESS
0-515-14235-2

WHEN DEPUTY U.S. MARSHAL CUSTIS LONG STOPS
A STAGECOACH ROBBERY, HE TRACKS THE BANDITS
TO A TOWN CALLED ZAMORA. A HAVEN FOR
THE LAWLESS, IT'S RULED BY ONE OF THE MOST
POWERFUL, BRILLIANT, AND BEAUTIFUL WOMEN
IN THE WEST...A WOMAN WHOM LONGARM WILL
HAVE TO FACE, UP CLOSE AND PERSONAL.

GIANT ACTION! GIANT ADVENTURE!

THE Gunsmith

GIANT

Giant Westerns featuring The Gunsmith

LITTLE SURESHOT AND THE WILD WEST SHOW
0-515-13851-7

DEAD WEIGHT
0-515-14028-7

RED MOUNTAIN
0-515-14206-9